He Was Asking

Shannon couldn't. She just couldn't ...
anger had permitted her to display herself
before the man. But Roman had no intention
of permitting her to escape. Catching her at
the door, he placed a restraining hand on her
arm and turned her around, pressing her
against the closed bedroom door as his lips
sought hers.

To her horror, Shannon felt herself move
forward to meet his embrace. She wanted him
to hold her. She wanted his lips to touch hers.
She knew it was insane, but she wanted
Roman Morgan!

BRENDA TRENT
has a life right out of romance. She followed her
heart from Virginia to California, where she
met the man of her dreams. With his encour-
agement she gave up working to concentrate on
another dream—writing—and we are proud to
introduce her work through Silhouette Romances.

Dear Reader:

Silhouette Romances is an exciting new publishing venture. We will be presenting the very finest writers of contemporary romantic fiction as well as outstanding new talent in this field. It is our hope that our stories, our heroes and our heroines will give you, the reader, all you want from romantic fiction.

Also, *you* play an important part in our future plans for Silhouette Romances. We welcome any suggestions or comments on our books and I invite you to write to us at the address below.

So, enjoy this book and all the wonderful romances from Silhouette. They're for *you!*

Karen Solem
Editor-in-Chief
Silhouette Books
P. O. Box 769
New York, N.Y. 10019

BRENDA TRENT
A Stranger's Wife

Silhouette *Romance*

Published by Silhouette Books New York

America's Publisher of Contemporary Romance

To my husband Robert who, over the years, has patiently read every single word of each manuscript.

Other Silhouette Romances by Brenda Trent

Rising Star
Winter Dreams

SILHOUETTE BOOKS, a Simon & Schuster Division of
GULF & WESTERN CORPORATION
1230 Avenue of the Americas, New York, N.Y. 10020

Copyright © 1981 by Brenda Trent

Distributed by Pocket Books

ISBN: 0-671-57110-9

First Silhouette Books printing October, 1981

10 9 8 7 6 5 4 3 2 1

America's Publisher of Contemporary Romance

Printed in the U.S.A.

A Stranger's
Wife

Chapter One

With the smell of salt water strong in her nostrils and a fine mist of ocean spray dampening her cheeks, Shannon stared broodingly at her surroundings. It was strange, she thought, how empty the beach seemed without Jarod.

Despite the brisk April afternoon winds, the beach was full of activity. Surfers braved the cold water and shell seekers searched the soft wet sands along the water's edge for beautiful, fascinating booty. Joggers clad in bright sweatsuits clocked their miles on the inconstant shore.

Shannon decided that she alone was shut out of the stream of life. Her world seemed to have ended when she lost Jarod. Sitting on the cool sand with her blue-sweatered arms wrapped around her long legs, black hair whipping away from her sun-browned face, she stared longingly at the sea until she lost all thought of time and place.

A volleyball sent a shower of sand over her pants as it landed heavily beside her, jolting her back to reality. She acknowledged the hasty apology as a tall, thin young man sheepishly retrieved the ball and rejoined his team. Life did go on, she thought, turning her attention back to the ocean. She marveled that she could listen to the waves and not weep for Jarod. She and the sea should be enemies, she reminded herself. The old pain seared across her mind as fresh and burning as it had the day she had heard the news.

Almost a year had passed since it happened—twelve long months since he had warmed her with his vitality—and yet it seemed like only yesterday. Here before her uncle's oceanfront home on the part of the beach they liked to call theirs, she and Jarod had shared many precious hours. She could still visualize every line of his long lean body. She could feel his chest pressed against her when he had hugged her close. She could still see his blond hair curled against his turned-up jacket collar as they strolled along the shore, his blue eyes bright.

But they were over now, those idyllic days, those dreams, that warmth of shared love. The same sea that had called them to frolic had claimed Jarod, refusing even to yield the strong, muscled body she had loved so well. Like a jealous lover, the sea had stolen him, smothered him, and kept him.

It didn't matter to Shannon what wrongdoing he was accused of, and it didn't matter that his case had been stamped "Presumed dead." Nor did it matter that his picture had been in every local newspaper with the ugly, chilling word "Suicide" heading it.

The vicious rumors and the sly whispers were not real to her. Her heart wouldn't accept his death as a suicide—he who had loved life to the fullest, he who had promised her the future. He was still alive in her heart, and somehow she couldn't quite believe that she would never see his broad, dimpled smile or the twinkle in his eyes again. Jarod's small, empty boat had washed ashore, broken and leaking, but no sign of him had been found. An older man who had been charged in the crime with him had jumped bail and vanished. The authorities were still searching for him. Shannon was sure the man had made Jarod the scapegoat. Jarod had protested bitterly that he had not been involved, and Shannon had believed him. She couldn't imagine him being capable of wrong-doing, any more than she could imagine him dead. Not her Jarod.

"Shannon Andrews?"

The voice callously intruding on her thoughts was cold, commanding and masculine. Shannon was compelled to turn toward it. Looking up at the tall man silhouetted against the last vestiges of a setting sun above the crest of the ocean, she saw that he was strikingly handsome, with broad shoulders and black wavy hair. His features were strong and dramatic, but as Shannon's eyes met his, she shivered. His face wore a mask of bitterness as he glared at her. His cold presence caused her to wrap her arms tighter about her legs to ward off the chill of his gaze.

"Yes?" Her mellow voice was hesitant. She resented the aloof stranger's invasion. He was cruel to disturb her thoughts of Jarod. And yet Shannon was aware that her attraction to this man's harsh good looks made her feel slightly breathless.

"I'm told you have rooms for rent. I want to see them." His stern gray eyes, topped by dark, uneven brows, stared at her levelly.

Not even so much as an "if I may," Shannon told herself. Her immediate reaction to this remote, demanding stranger was to deny that she had rooms available. But after all, she reminded herself practically, she was a businesswoman now, and her livelihood depended on keeping the rooms occupied. Her parents had been killed in a boating accident when she was eighteen, and she had gone to live with her mother's brother. Now that her uncle was dead and Jarod was missing, she was alone in the world. She had never expected it. Even though her uncle had

thought Jarod irresponsible, she had counted on him
sharing her life. She found it hard to be indepen-
dent. Every penny had to be budgeted, and the
season when strangers begged for her rooms
wouldn't start for a few more weeks, yet her finan-
cial situation demanded that she keep them rented
year round.

The old Dutch house her uncle had willed her a
year and a half ago had been a wonderful gift, and
she had taken possession of it joyfully. But she was
hardly a member of the idle rich. After giving up her
job in the bank where she and Jarod had worked, she
had more freedom than most young women who
were self-supporting, but the taxes along the beach-
front were high. And yet she could never sell the
property she loved. She and Jarod had planned to
spend their lives in the old house.

One day he might come back to her, and she had
to be there in their house where he could find her.
Nightly she prayed that he had been rescued and that
he was safe. Anything was possible in such a case,
wasn't it? Perhaps he had been picked up by a ship
that had later been wrecked on a coastal island.
Perhaps it was impossible for him to make his way
back to her. Maybe he had amnesia. She had to
believe that he was safe somewhere. She had to.

The sharp snapping of a finger and a thumb
riveted her floundering thoughts to the stranger's
granite face. It was, Shannon thought resentfully,
almost as though he were commanding an animal to
pay attention to him.

"The rooms, Miss Andrews. The rooms," he
growled impatiently. "If you have none available,
say so, but don't waste my time. And please don't
doze in my presence."

"I was not dozing," she retorted irritably, her

green eyes blazing. "I have a lot on my mind, and I was thinking about . . . about the rooms."

"Quite a chore for you apparently," he muttered, frowning down at her.

Well, he certainly had some nerve. Just who did he think he was to speak to her like that? Angered, she stood up and began to brush the sand from her blue terry pants but found that she had been sitting cross-legged much too long and her legs were unstable. Awkwardly she stumbled forward on numb, tingling legs and suddenly sprawled on her hands and knees, her rear jutting up in a most unladylike fashion. Her face burning, she looked up into the man's face and was astonished to see that he didn't make the slightest attempt to offer her aid.

His muscular arms were folded over his broad chest. He stood motionless and stared at her while she made an idiot of herself. "Been walking long?" he murmured in a low tone, his gaze traveling boldly down her body.

"Well . . . you rude . . . well, I never in my life saw the likes of you, mister!" she muttered, struggling to make her legs do her bidding. Her eyes glared into the stranger's mocking gray ones. Defiantly she managed to get up, only to fall backward, legs crumpling beneath her as she landed once again in the sand.

Surprisingly gentle hands grasped her arms and lifted her, like a piece of inert baggage, from her seated position. "Thank you," she said with chilly deliberation, shaking her legs to restore the circulation and yanking her arms from his hands with a hard downward motion. "I hope I didn't inconvenience you too much." When her bright eyes glanced up to meet his, she realized that he was several inches taller than her five feet, six inches.

A taunting half-smile moved his full lips, causing a faint brightening in his icy eyes. "Only if you don't have rooms available. Then I might as well have thrown my time to the wind rather than waste it here with you."

Infuriated by his remark, she beckoned sharply to him, and marched determinedly toward the house, her shoeless feet sinking deep into the sand as she stalked away. She didn't turn to look, but she knew he was behind her. Not that she cared, she told herself, if he followed or not. There would soon be other renters for her rooms if he didn't take them now. She wasn't so desperate that she wanted to put up with him! Shannon wasn't at all sure that she could stand to be under the same roof with such a barbarian.

Charging rudely across the front patio without checking her steps, she rushed into the front hall. Apparently he had kept pace with her, because she heard him murmur, "Wonderful. I hoped this would be the house. It was my first choice."

Shannon opened the door to her apartment with a key from her pocket and reached for the key to the vacant rooms. Starting up the stairs to the apartment over hers, she made no reply to his comment. But even as angry as she was, she recognized the charm of the house, and she could understand his interest in it. Although it wasn't the most handsome struc-ture in the neighborhood, it had a certain character that set it apart.

Blue Haven was perfectly named. The huge old house, painted a deep blue, trimmed in white, its sliding glass patio doors and wide front door giving it a happy, welcome look, stood as a warm shelter from life's storms. It was a delightful blend of old and new, and Shannon took great pride in it.

Bougainvillea vines climbed to the roof, their flowers a splash of scarlet against a blue background. A white picket fence marked off the front patio, and half-barrels filled with trailing flowers scattered color across the used brick. The house was sectioned into four apartments so that each had a grand view of the silver-blue waters of the Pacific Ocean. Each room commanded a high rent during the season by sheer virtue of location.

Newport Beach was California's playground for the idle rich and the poor beach lover alike. In summer people flocked to the beach to sunbathe, enjoy the water, visit the Dory Fishing Fleet, stroll about Newport Pier, and roam in and out of the shops and long-established restaurants. There was always a waiting list for the local housing. The working populace saved for years to be able to stay three weeks in an oceanfront apartment for one never-to-be forgotten summer, while the wealthy spent huge sums of money for the season and never missed a cent. It was spring now and soon the warm waters and the sand would call out to the myriad beach lovers hungrily seeking out living quarters.

She would be turning people away, Shannon mused, instead of showing rooms to arrogant men like this one following her. She turned the key and shoved the door open. When she turned to the man, however, she discovered that he wasn't behind her after all. Glancing down the stairs, she saw that he stood at the bottom, one foot on the first step as he leaned against the banister, staring up at her.

"Perhaps you would rather have your husband show me the rooms," he drawled lazily.

"The house is mine!" Shannon snapped. "I don't have a husband. Do you want to see the rooms or not?" Her lips tightened into a thin line of irritation and she reached for the doorknob, ready to shut the door.

"I should have known—about the husband, I mean," he commented flatly, walking slowly up the steps.

Shannon crossed her arms impatiently. She waited until he reached the top step before she walked into the living room. "This is it—bedroom, living room and kitchen. You have to share the bath at the end of the hall with the other upstairs tenant," she stated, her bright eyes smoldering with flecks of amber. "Three hundred and ten dollars a month. Take it or leave it. In a few weeks the rent goes up to three hundred a week."

Undaunted by that information, he stared calmly at her for a few seconds before walking over to peer out the window at the sandy beaches yielding to the descending dusk. "It's beautiful," he murmured more to himself than to her. "I'll take it."

"Oh," she said, startled by his abrupt decision. "Don't you want to inspect the kitchen and the bedroom?"

"No."

His refusal annoyed her. She had done some redecorating when the house had become hers, and she was proud of the rooms. Her uncle had seen fit to provide the tenants with good furniture, much of it old-fashioned but attractive. She had played on the antique theme, adding baskets, feathers, paintings and wallpaper. But obviously the man cared nothing about all that.

"Then you only have to sign a lease and you can move in. If you'll come to my apartment, it will only take a minute," she said crisply. "With the three hundred ten in advance, there's a security deposit of one hundred and fifty and a key deposit of three dollars. Close the door after you," she ordered. Not bothering to look to see if he followed, she went down the steps and opened the door to her own apartment.

She always felt contented when she entered her rooms. Her living room was decorated with wicker furniture, bright cushions and a big white comfortable couch. An antique trunk she had spent many hours refurbishing sat before the couch, and Victorian tables covered with homemade scarves stood in front of her sliding glass patio door. Tall plants gave the room a lush appearance, and the walls were adorned with a few amateur paintings of bright flowers in buckets and milk cans.

She heard his step as he entered, and she turned to find him studying the room critically, as if it were in dire need of his approval or disapproval. He certainly hadn't looked at his own apartment with such careful scrutiny. His penetrating gray eyes settled on the paintings.

"Are you a painter, too?" he asked, looking at her at last and making the question something just short of an insult.

"No," she said succinctly, telling herself that he must think himself very important. Was he an authority on painters? She didn't care what he thought; she had taken an instant dislike to him and she felt no need to indulge his sudden desire for conversation.

"Who did those?" he persisted. Again his question was somehow derogatory. Jarod had painted the colorful bouquets of daisies, roses and poppies on the weathered boards of old grape crates. She was fiercely protective of his childlike but unadulterated talent.

"Someone dear to me," she replied, raising her

sea-green eyes to meet the steel-gray of his. "I gather from your tone that you find them rather amateurish."

"My tone, as you call it, didn't indicate that I found them anything at all. I merely asked who the artist was. I realize that every man sees the world through different eyes. The painter of the boards captured what he saw rather skillfully in a primitive manner. I thought you might be the artist."

With a questioning look, she scanned his strong features. The identity of the artist was none of his business, she declared silently. Then she realized that she was being silly. After all, he was just making conversation, even if he had that annoying way of sounding as if he knew it all. Besides, she reminded herself, Jarod couldn't really have been called an artist even if the paintings he had done were among her most treasured possessions.

"I don't paint," she said, turning so that she could look at the paintings. "My fiancé painted them at my request. Painting was a hobby which he found very relaxing and fulfilling."

The stranger placed a hand to his strong chin. "I see," he said, watching her with thoughtful, unfathomable eyes. "Did you ever pose for him?"

"He didn't do portraits," she retorted shortly. Shaking her head to free herself from the haunting thoughts of Jarod, she walked over to the stately mahogany desk that sat in the corner of the room. Reaching out a slim hand, she picked up a rental agreement. "Do you know how long you'll be staying?" she asked, turning her eyes to his face.

"Do you need to know?" His terse question seemed to imply that it was none of her business.

"Well, yes. Yes," she replied firmly. Just who did he think he was? After all, she was renting him the rooms in her home! Of course she needed to know.

His eyes moved to the sea beyond the window. His voice was pensive and remote when he spoke. "Probably until June. I hate the crowds, and summer is sure to bring them out."

"Of course the crowds come in the summer months," she agreed. "The beach is public." He probably doesn't have the money to stay in the summer season, she mused. The thought made her feel strangely smug, and she was surprised that she should feel happy to know that he wasn't well-off. She knew how it felt to pinch pennies, but then, she had never tried to be anything more than she was. He was obviously assuming airs. "Name?" she asked.

"Morgan—Roman Morgan."

"Permanent address?"

"Does it matter?"

Placing her hands on her hips in irritation, she glared at him. "No, I suppose not," she snapped, making very little attempt to conquer her annoyance. She liked to have a permanent address in case of tenant damage, but she hadn't had any serious problems since the house had become hers. Most people who rented the apartments spent the majority of their time on the beach or traveling about the area enjoying such magic places as Disneyland, Knotts Berry Farm, Movieland Wax Museum and a host of other recreational centers.

"Do you object to signing the forms?" she inquired tartly. "Or to paying the money?"

A half-smile played across his lips. "I always object to paying out money, Miss Andrews, but there are times when it's a necessity."

"Is how you make your living a secret, Mr. Morgan?" she asked derisively.

"I'm an artist."

So! she told herself. Another poor artist! She

watched as he signed the form she handed him. She couldn't resist one more question. "What do you paint, Mr. Morgan?"

"Are you interested in buying?" His gray eyes mocked her.

"Well, no. Of course not."

"Then you're not really interested in my work. You're just curious about my ability to pay the rent. Isn't that it?"

Pressing her lips tightly together, she tried to resist the blush that colored her cheeks. "Yes. And please pay on time. The rent is due the first of each month, even though you're moving in on the seventh." She watched as he pulled his wallet from his back pocket and counted out the money. "Here's your copy of the agreement," she stated as he laid the money on her desk. Stalking to the front door, she held it open, hoping that he would take the hint and leave.

As though he enjoyed provoking her, he strolled toward her, stopping much too near when he reached the door. Pulling two keys from her pocket, she set one on a table and slapped his into his open palm. "Your key."

His large hand closed down on hers as he reached for the key. She saw the aggressive move and tried to evade it by jerking her hand back, but she was too late. His hand had made a prisoner of hers.

"Are you always so easily aroused?" he murmured unexpectedly, his eyes sparkling with new life at her discomfort.

"Let go of my hand, Mr. Morgan," she snapped, unable to imagine why her heart was pounding so violently. "You only get three rooms for your money, not the right to fondle me."

Suddenly he dropped her hand as if it had burned him. "Fondle you?" he repeated. "I hardly call that fondling, Miss Andrews. You have a very strong imagination."

"Why, you insufferable . . ." Shannon clamped her lips together and ran a hand through her dark hair. Resisting an impulse to yank the rental agreement from his hand and rip it into a hundred pieces, she announced, "We've finished with our business. Please leave."

"With pleasure." Raising a hand to his head in a mock salute, he strolled from the room. When she had slammed the door loudly behind him, Shannon leaned against it, trying to catch her breath. Closing her eyes and sighing in relief, she remained perfectly still for a couple of minutes. She didn't know why she had rented the apartment to that man. No one had forced her to.

A sharp rap from the other side caused her to jerk her head away from the door. "Yes?" she called out in a shaky voice.

"May I speak with you?" The deep voice fairly growled at her.

"What do you want now?" she grumbled. She was beginning to get the feeling that the man was more interested in her than in his apartment.

She was unable to miss the disgust in his voice. "I don't talk to doors."

"I hope you don't make me regret renting to you, Mr. Morgan," she replied, clenching her hands. "I have no intention of opening my door again. Our business is finished. Say whatever you wish to me and let me get on with my evening."

"I need another key, Miss Andrews," he snarled.

"One key is all you get from me." She gritted her teeth in anger, listening for a further comment from him.

When there was only silence from the other side of

the door, she sighed. Maybe he had decided to go away.

As she turned, relieved, to prepare her dinner, she reached absently into her pocket and noticed that her key was missing. "What did I do with it?" she muttered aloud. Hastily she searched her apartment, but she couldn't remember where she had put it. Oh, well. It didn't matter now; she had an extra. She slipped it into her pocket and went to the kitchen to make dinner. She would find the key tomorrow. It had to be in the living room somewhere; she remembered removing both keys from her pocket when she handed Roman his. She was simply too exhausted from her dealings with him to track it down now.

After she had eaten, she slipped into her nightgown, picked up a favorite book and climbed into bed. After reading for a while, she let the familiar words lull her to sleep. And for the first time in weeks, she fell asleep without crying over Jarod.

At about ten-thirty, she awakened with a start. For a few tense moments she wasn't sure if she had been dreaming or if she had actually heard a noise in the front room. Eyes wide open and heart thudding, she fought an impulse to hide under the covers as she had done when she was a child. Cautiously she raised herself up in bed, straining to hear any foreign sound. She had always worried about burglars, living in a resort area, but so far neither she nor her tenants had been bothered. She held her breath, listening for a few frightening seconds, hearing nothing but the comforting ticking of her old mantel clock. When a few moments had crept by, she dared to breathe a bit easier. She tentatively made her way to the front room on legs that were only slightly shaky. Standing in the living room in the dark, unwilling to turn on a light for fear of what she might see, she finally decided that everything seemed to be in order. There were few places for an intruder to hide, and no one had jumped out to grab her. Feeling a bit braver, she walked into the kitchen and turned on a small overhead lamp. Nothing seemed amiss. It must have been the wind, a prowling animal or the strong imagination which Roman Morgan had made an allusion to. Roman Morgan! That must have been it, she thought, as a picture of him flashed through her mind. He might have made the noise above her. He certainly didn't seem like the type to consider other people. Shaking her head as she switched off the light, she went back to her bed and climbed in. As she fluffed her pillow and rolled over on her side, Roman's dark face surfaced to taunt her. With him in her thoughts, she drifted back to sleep.

It could have been only a few minutes later that she turned restlessly in her sleep, prodded awake by the feeling that something still wasn't right. Something or someone actually seemed to have settled into the bed beside her, the weight causing the mattress to ease down a bit. She rolled over on her back, knowing that she must be dreaming and trying to shake the troublesome sensation. Eyes still closed as she refused to dignify the crazy thought by actually looking for trouble, she stretched out a hand to reassure herself that all was well. Her hand trailed down a hard, warm, hairy chest. Gasping in fright, she flung back the covers and jumped out of bed, frantically flipping on the light as she did so. She simply couldn't believe what she saw. Roman Morgan was lying in her bed!

Her heart pounding savagely, she glared down at him. "What on earth do you think you're doing?" she spluttered, eyes full of rage and indignation. "What are you doing in my bed?"

Dressed in pajama bottoms, he stared levelly at her from his hooded gray eyes as he reached for the cover and pulled it back up.

"Well?" she demanded, too shocked to be afraid.

"I'm sleepy," he drawled, stifling a pretended yawn. "I'm going to bed."

"How did you get in here?" she shrieked. "Get out right now! Get out of my rooms and get out of this building! If you so much as set foot on my premises again, I'll call the police. Get out! I never in my life—" she began.

"You never what?" he interrupted, eyeing her closely. "Gave your key to another tenant?"

"What are you talking about?" she gasped, jumping back as if he had slapped her.

Deliberately pausing to boldly scan her scantily clad body, he murmured, "You know what I'm talking about."

"I do not!" she insisted, wanting to hide from the look in those hard eyes.

Before she knew what was happening, his hands reached out. She didn't have time to jump away as he grabbed her and pulled her down on top of him. He gripped the hair at the nape of her neck and forced her lips to meet his in a brutal kiss. Twisting and turning, she tried desperately to escape him, but he held her too tightly. His eyes looked into hers when he ended the kiss.

"I mean," he murmured in a husky voice, his breath warm on her face, "I thought you intended for me to share your apartment—and your bed. You did give me your key. And I did pay 'rent.' What else was I to think?"

"You're crazy!" she hissed, staring at him with blazing eyes. She was painfully aware of his body beneath hers. She felt as if she were on fire, and her heart wouldn't stop its erratic pounding. She was shocked to realize that her response wasn't one of fear. His nearness sent her senses reeling as even Jarod never had.

"You . . . you get out of here!" she repeated. "I'm warning you. The minute you let me go, I'll phone the police and have you arrested for breaking and entering . . . and . . . and assaulting me!"

A slow smile spread over the lips that had so recently touched hers, and she couldn't stop herself from looking down at them. "Then I'll have to hold you on top of me all night, won't I? Besides," he drawled, "I do have a key to your apartment. I'm sure the police will think the same thing I did."

Her eyes opened wide and she blinked rapidly. "What do you mean?"

He shrugged his broad shoulders. "What else? That your fiancé was neglecting you, if, indeed, there really is a fiancé, and you wanted me in your bed."

"You animal!" she breathed into his face. "Let me go!" Tossing her head back, she wiggled against him, only to succeed in making herself even more aware of his hard, muscled body.

"After all," he pointed out dryly, oblivious to her struggle, his hands holding her tightly against his body, "I did try to tell you that you had given me the wrong key, but you . . . pretended not to understand." His taunting eyes stared into hers.

Helplessly she stared back. What else could she do? He had tried to tell her about the key, hadn't he? Somehow she had given him the key to her apartment! How on earth had she managed to do that? No wonder she hadn't been able to find her key.

"I . . . I beg your pardon," she stammered. "I can understand how you might have gotten the wrong idea, but it was all a mistake. Please just let me up. I can explain it." She tried to move away from him, acutely aware of his arms locked around her like steel bands, pressing her soft curves to his hard body. She knew that his key had been in her pocket, as well as her own. She remembered removing them when she had given him the rental agreement. That was it! She must have kept his key and given him hers by mistake.

"You didn't really mean to give me your key?" he queried in mock surprise, a hint of a smile twisting his lips.

Taking a deep breath, she declared indignantly, "Indeed I did not. If you'll just let me up from here, I'll find you the right key."

"Pity," he drawled. "I was just beginning to get comfortable."

Comfortable! she thought, confronting her own feelings. She found his presence unaccountably tantalizing, cruelly attractive and provocative, anything but comfortable. He released her and she struggled quickly away.

"I really am sorry that you've been inconvenienced," she murmured apologetically, "but surely you can't believe that I intended for you to share my bed." Feeling an inexplicable shiver of excitement at the very thought, she rubbed her arms briskly before lacing her fingers together in front of her.

His lips curved into a cynical smile. "Of course not, but you were so pigheaded about letting me explain my problem that I thought you deserved to be taught a lesson."

Pigheaded indeed! she thought. She had a few names for him, too, but she felt it best to just get rid of him. "You nearly frightened me to death," she accused, turning to leave the room.

She heard him laugh, and his words followed her.

"If you'd been that frightened, you would have called out to the other roomers."

She angrily flipped on all the lights along her way, wondering just how much truth there was in his statement. She had been scared out of her wits until she saw that it was Roman lying beside her. Then she had simply been furious. When she crossed the living room, she was shocked to see his luggage sitting on the floor. He really had some nerve! Trying to hide her exasperation, she searched her desk for his key. She couldn't seem to find it anywhere. Seeing him trail into the room after her, she looked about frantically. Where could she have put it? Just by chance, she saw it lying on the table by the door and hurried over to get it.

"Here it is," she muttered thickly, turning around to look at him. Her face turned crimson. He looked so exposed, standing there in his pajama bottoms, his broad hairy chest tapering to a lean waist. Finishing her hasty examination, her eyes met his and she saw his amusement. "Please get dressed," she said, averting her eyes with difficulty. "I don't want anyone to see you leaving my apartment like that."

"Why not?" he teased.

"Really, you are the most . . ." she began, turning toward him. When she saw him pick up his slacks and shirt from the couch and start to pull them on, she turned away again. He must already have been undressed and standing in the bedroom when she was first awakened. In a minute he stepped in front of her, holding her key in one hand while he reached for his with the other. She slapped the key into his open palm, quickly drawing her hand away to hold it out for her own key.

A wicked smile curved his lips. "I'll keep this one

if you want me to. Don't let me shame you into taking it back."

"I've had enough of you for one day, Mr. Morgan," she insisted tartly. "I never intended for you to have a key to my apartment, and you know it."

"Why don't you call me Roman?" he suggested. "I feel that I know you so well already." His eyes shifted over her nightdress, and she realized for the first time that she was almost as exposed as he had been. As she crossed her arms, she heard him laugh. "It's Shannon, isn't it?"

"It is not!" she declared. "To you, it's Miss Andrews!"

"I see." He let the key drop from his hand, and Shannon watched, appalled, as it fell to the floor. She refused to pick it up while he stood there gloating.

"I'm afraid I've made a terrible mistake in renting to you, Mr. Morgan," she said in a tight little voice. "Why don't you occupy the apartment tonight and then leave tomorrow morning. I'll be happy to return every cent of your money if you'll just go away."

His eyes were hard and cold as they met hers. "We have a contract, Miss Andrews, and I've done nothing to invalidate it. I intend to occupy the apartment until June." Abruptly he picked up his suitcase and left the room. He turned back to look through the open door. "And, Miss Andrews, if I had really assaulted you, you would have known it."

She rushed to slam the door, but he closed it before she got there. Not until she had picked up her key and dropped into a chair did she realize how shaken she was. She would live to regret renting the apartment to that man. Of that fact she was certain, but it was too late now. Thank heaven he was only staying a couple of months. She sighed as she heard his tread on the stairs, counting them one by one until she heard him open his door and enter the room. For a moment she wished the house was carpeted, but it just wasn't practical with so many beachgoers tracking sand in all day long. She sighed again.

The apartment above her consisted of three rooms in a row over her own three. Across the hall from her were the rooms of a red-haired writer, Shirle Wayne. Above Shirle's rooms were those of Carmen Angel, an elderly woman who lived with her small dog, Pansy. Shannon thought how fortunate she was that Shirle and Mrs. Angel lived with her year round. She didn't have to go through the annoying inconvenience of renting out their rooms each season. Shirle, a murder-mystery writer, had been in the house for several years. Although Mrs. Angel had lived there permanently for only two years, she and her husband had stayed in the house each summer since their marriage four decades ago. Now widowed, but luckily well off, Mrs. Angel had confided her intention of remaining at Blue Haven no matter how high the cost of the apartment rose. She said that her fondest memories were of the old Dutch house, and she didn't want to live anywhere else.

Shannon heard the bedsprings squeak upstairs as Roman settled in, and she closed her eyes. Why, oh why, did he have to rent the apartment over hers? She was sure he was going to destroy the tranquillity of her life. His manner was so arrogant, and his presence was so . . . so disturbing.

Chapter Two

The bright morning sun awakened Shannon, causing her to stretch and yawn before swinging her legs over the side of the bed. She was surprised to hear heavy steps overhead until she remembered her new tenant. She had somehow managed to suppress all thoughts of him during the long night. She didn't care if she ever saw him again. She should have rented the rooms to a woman.

Artists! she thought contemptuously. Shirle was moody, but she certainly wasn't surly and snide like Roman. Sometimes Shirle went for weeks without speaking a single word to anyone, but at other times she dropped in for coffee and chatter or sat on the beach sunning with Shannon. Shannon liked the tall, vital young woman, but she felt that she could never make a real friend of her because of that uncertain artistic temperament.

Their meeting had been fortunate. When Shannon had taken over the house, Shirle's regular typist had just quit to get married and Shannon had gotten the job. The house and the money she earned from Shirle made it possible for her to stay at home instead of taking an outside job as she had feared she would have to do when she had quit working at the bank. She simply hadn't been able to stay on at the bank, facing the stares and the pitiful looks. But, of course, she had had to earn money. Because she wanted Jarod's name cleared, and because she couldn't accept his death without proof, she had hired a private detective to search for him. The cost was high, but her love for him wouldn't allow her to give up. So far the detective hadn't found anything, but she had no intention of abandoning the hunt even though the detective, Sam Harvard, was requesting more money as time dragged on.

Shannon pulled her housecoat around her shoulders and ran a hand through her long dark hair on the way to the bathroom she shared with Shirle. She knew it would be empty; Shirle wrote until the early-morning hours and slept most of the day. Opening her door, she trudged sleepily down the hall. Just as she reached the bath, Roman stepped out of it—dressed in a towel!

"You can't use this bath!" Shannon sputtered. "This is mine and the downstairs tenant's. What do you think you're doing?"

Roman crossed his arms over his chest, and Shannon's eyes were drawn to the mat of thick dark hair, some of it still damp. "I had no idea it would disturb you so, Miss Andrews. The upstairs bath was occupied, and I wanted to take my shower and get on with life. I have to bring the rest of my belongings in from the car, and I want to paint today. Do pardon me if I've breached the etiquette of this household," he said sarcastically. His eyes were cynical and taunting, and Shannon felt ashamed that she had lashed out at him so harshly. The tenants often used whichever bath was available, but she hadn't expected to see him this morning, hadn't wanted to see him. She remembered his hard body lying beneath hers on her bed, and she flushed. Clearing her throat, she tried to meet his piercing gaze.

"It . . . it doesn't matter," she conceded, trying to keep her eyes on his face. Seeing him standing there nearly nude, she had the wildest desire to be held in his arms. It was ridiculous! She had never felt that way about any man but Jarod.

"Dozing again, Miss Andrews?" he murmured.

Shannon realized that she had been staring at the towel he wore, and she felt her cheeks burn. What on earth was the matter with her? She was twenty-two years old, not some star-struck teenager, and she was heartsick over Jarod's disappearance. How could this arrogant man distract her so? She hadn't wanted any man but Jarod since she was eighteen, and she had never permitted him to take her to bed. She was old-fashioned enough to have wanted everything to be right and special when they married. And here she was thinking all kinds of tantalizing thoughts about this man standing before her. She shook her head. The worry and strain of the last twelve months had taken their toll. She was so lost without Jarod.

"I'm sorry," she murmured. Roman Morgan was going to live in her house for several months. She had to curb her feelings about him—all her feelings. Attempting a smile, she said, "I'm not awake yet. Haven't had my coffee."

Solemn-faced, he nodded. "Will you have a cup with me? I left the pot brewing."

"No. No, thank you, Mr. . . . . Roman," she was quick to reply. "Perhaps another time."

Unexpectedly he reached out to her hair, allowing his long fingers to fan through the dark strands. Shannon drew back defensively, ready to tell him to keep his hands off her, but he produced a bit of lint and handed it to her. Nodding again, he turned to climb the steps as Shannon put her hand on the bathroom door to open it. She heard him call down, "There will be another time, Shannon. You can be sure of it."

She rushed into the bathroom and quickly shut the

door. He was so sure of himself! He seemed to be able to read her thoughts, she thought irritably as the masculine smell of shaving lotion teased her nostrils in the steamy room. It was strange to have had a man in her bathroom, and she felt a little excited as she stripped and climbed into the shower. Thinking of Roman bathing naked in her shower just minutes ago sent a shiver up her spine. With a toss of her head, she forced the thought away.

After her shower, Shannon busied herself in her apartment, but she couldn't keep her thoughts off Roman. She could hear him as he came and went, taking possessions in and arranging them. She had a new manuscript of Shirle's to type, and she forced herself to sit and work at the typewriter.

The typing kept her busy until lunchtime, when she took a break for a sandwich and a cup of coffee. After she returned to the living room, she opened the drapes of her sliding glass door for the first time that morning. She was surprised to see Roman, shoeless, dressed in cut-off jeans and a sweatshirt, standing on the beach in front of the house. A voluptuous woman stood before him, occasionally throwing back her head to laugh at some comment of his. Shannon watched for a couple of minutes, then yanked the drapery closed. What that man did was of no concern to her. Striding back to her old typewriter, she began to pound on the keys, working off the hostility she felt toward her new roomer. It was only a few minutes later that she heard the woman speaking to Roman as they made their way upstairs. Shannon stalked to her front door and put her ear close to it, fuming. She had known it was a mistake to rent to that man; already he was entertaining a woman in his rooms. He would probably have them coming and going at all hours of the night.

As the afternoon wore on, she tried to concentrate on her typing, but she found herself unable to ignore the purring feminine voice and the occasional high laughter from above. Her heart almost stopped when she heard Roman's deep, smooth voice. His guest seemed to be staying an inordinately long time. By four o'clock Shannon could sit at the typewriter no longer. Restless, she seemed naturally drawn to the upper portion of the house, deciding in the end to visit with Mrs. Angel. She told herself that she wanted to spend a pleasant half-hour with the old lady, but she couldn't deny the fact that her curiosity about Roman's visitor was really what drove her upstairs. Perhaps she might hear their conversation more clearly from Mrs. Angel's rooms. She despised snoops, but she simply couldn't help herself.

She walked up the steps very slowly. Seeing Roman's door closed, she went across the hall and tapped on Mrs. Angel's and felt a momentary surge of guilt at the delighted expression on the old woman's face when she opened the door.

"Shannon, my dear, how nice to see you," she exclaimed, beaming. "Pansy and I thought you'd forgotten your old friends up here."

Shannon smiled warmly at her, thinking how accurate the woman's name was. The angelic, wrinkled old face was topped by a cap of wispy gray curls. Mrs. Angel's small, bright, dark eyes twinkled with joy, reflecting her friendly personality. More than a few times, she and Shannon had shared dinner and a pleasant evening. She was always there to listen when Shannon was feeling especially low about Jarod.

"Do come in," Mrs. Angel said, placing a weathered hand on Shannon's arm to urge her forward. "How are you today?"

When Shannon entered, Pansy, a fluffy white poodle, bounded from the couch and jumped excitedly about in front of her. Shannon reached down to take the little dog in her arms. "How are you, Pansy?" she asked, playfully rubbing the panting dog's head. Setting the dog free as she turned to Mrs. Angel, she said, "I wanted to tell you that we have a new roomer."

Mrs. Angel sat down on the couch and indicated a spot beside her. "Oh, yes, my dear, I saw him. Handsome, isn't he?"

Shannon shrugged as if she hadn't noticed. "I suppose—if you like that type. I haven't really paid that much attention to him, myself." She was surprised that she felt the need to lie. Of course she had noticed how handsome Roman was. How could she not have? "He's an artist," she added, not wanting to linger on his looks.

"An artist. How very romantic."

At just that moment, Shannon heard a high giggle from his rooms, and she raised her eyebrows in irritation. "He seems to fancy himself quite a ladies' man."

"Sounds like my Leon," the woman remarked, smiling reminiscently. "Oh, my dear, you should have seen my young man when he was in his twenties. Why, the girls couldn't leave him alone. He was so handsome, dark like your new roomer, and a real charmer, he was."

Shannon smiled, but she was surprised that she found her thoughts wandering as Mrs. Angel talked about Leon. There had been numerous other times when Shannon had listened intently as he was lovingly discussed, but this afternoon she found that she was unable to concentrate on the woman's chatter. She didn't understand what had gotten into her since Roman had come here. She couldn't seem to keep her mind off him, although she found his personality thoroughly disagreeable. She rushed to tell herself that she certainly wasn't attracted to him in the least, even if he was handsome.

When she finally returned to her own apartment, after dinner with Mrs. Angel, it was getting dark. Sometime before she and Mrs. Angel had eaten dessert, she had heard Roman's guest leave, and she didn't hear him overhead when she went into her living room. She actually found herself straining to hear movements from above. Annoyed, she flipped the button to turn on the television, turning the sound up quite high, but soon found that she couldn't concentrate on the program. Having never cared much for television anyway except to watch the late talk shows, she switched the set off and wandered back to her typewriter, but that held her attention only briefly. In desperation she opened her sliding glass door and stepped out onto her private patio. Roman's balcony was directly above her, and since she hadn't heard him in his rooms, she was startled when she saw a shadow darken the brick in front of her. With a jolt she realized that Roman must be outside, leaning on the rail as he contemplated night falling on the ocean.

Her attention was attracted to a shapely young woman walking briskly down the sidewalk on tall heels that tapped with each step. When she passed under the streetlight, head tilted upward to stare at the houses, Shannon was able to get a good look at her. Dressed in a sleek blue suit with a fancy blouse showing beneath the open jacket, she looked very well-to-do. Her hair was neatly and stylishly done up on her head, and the hand that clutched a smart bag had long red nails that shimmered in the light. Suddenly the woman stopped, gasping as she stared at Blue Haven. Shannon stepped backward involuntarily, startled by the cry that came from the woman's red lips. "Roman!" the blonde called out, excitedly waving a hand.

Watching in fascination, she saw the beauty turn and run toward the house. Shannon pressed herself against the side of the door and stared as the woman hurried past, her heels tapping as she climbed the steps to the upper apartments. For a minute Shannon heard nothing else but the desperate knocking on Roman's door. She was certain now that it had been a mistake to rent to him, but how was she to know that he would have a stream of women at his door? The knocking continued, getting even louder when Roman didn't respond. Of course, Shannon knew he was there, as did the woman, and she slipped back inside and sneaked over to her door to open it. Why didn't he answer the woman's knock?

She listened as the sweet female voice pleaded, "Please, Roman. Please. This isn't solving anything. Let me in. I must talk to you."

Intrigued, Shannon opened her door a tiny bit wider, justifying her curiosity by telling herself that she had to know what went on in her home. The pleading intensified.

"Roman. Roman. I know you're in there. I saw you on the balcony. Roman," the woman begged, "let me in. I followed you all the way from Monterey and I've searched for you all day. Please, Roman. There are so many things that you don't understand. Oh, Roman. Don't do this to me. To us."

Shannon was surprised by the hammering of her own heart. What did she care that this woman was obviously intimately involved with her new tenant? Their apparent lovers' quarrel was none of her concern.

For a moment the hallway was quiet, and Shannon heard nothing but silence from the upstairs rooms.

The hiatus was only momentary. "Roman, for pity's sake," the woman said in a tense voice. "Roman." A sob caught in her throat and she moaned softly. As her anguish increased, she knocked harder, and Shannon's heart beat stronger in response. The noise was surely bothering her other tenants, but she couldn't bring herself to intercede as the drama intensified. "Roman!" the woman cried in a loud voice.

Shannon heard the door open abruptly and Roman's harsh voice growled, "Leave me alone. Stop harassing me, Elleen. I've nothing else to say to you, so get out of my life!"

The door slammed sharply and Shannon jumped. His cold bitter tone had chilled her. She almost hated him for the way he was treating the woman, and she didn't even know the situation.

"Open this door, Roman," the woman demanded, pounding incessantly. "You can't just end it like this!" Her voice was suddenly shrill. "It wasn't my fault. I won't let you forget me. Not after all we've meant to each other!"

"Keep your voice down!" Roman demanded in a low angry tone as the door opened again.

"I don't care who hears me," Elleen insisted. "All I care about is us! Oh, Roman, please let me explain. I know you'll understand if you'll just listen to me."

"It's a little late for that," he snapped, "but apparently it's the only way to silence you."

Shannon heard the woman step inside and the door bang closed. Only a few minutes later she heard Roman's angry command, "Get out!"

The door opened and Elleen fled. Shannon couldn't imagine why she felt so sorry for the pretty young woman. She didn't even know her, but having experienced Roman's cruel behavior herself, she could well imagine how terrible it would be to fall in

love with him as Elleen apparently had done. Shannon was glad her heart had already been given to
Jarod. She could imagine how painful it would be to
have it battered and bruised by a man like Roman
Morgan.

For a few minutes all was quiet upstairs. Then, to
Shannon's surprise, Roman's heavy steps followed
the woman's down the stairs. Watching from her
patio window, Shannon expected to see him pursue
Elleen. Instead, she saw him peel off his shoes and
shirt as he passed beneath the streetlight. She barely
made out his form as he charged across the sand and
slipped into the dark ocean.

Shannon felt cold all over, and her heart filled
with fear. All she could think of was the night waters
swallowing Jarod. Did Roman mean to take his life
out there in the dark sea? Blindly she tore after
Roman, shedding her slacks on the sand in the
process.

She rushed into the sea behind him, plunging into
the icy waters and feeling a numbing shock as the
cold sea engulfed her. She could hardly see Roman's
head as he stroked away from the shore. Forcing her
arms to churn as fast as she possibly could in the
black waters, she pursued him. It took her a couple
of frantic minutes to catch up with him. Breathless,
her heart and body working savagely, she panted,
"Stop, Roman! Stop! Nothing is worth throwing
away your life! Come back. We'll talk about it!" She
couldn't make out the expression on his face as he
turned to look at her, but she intuitively knew that
he resented her intervention.

"What are you doing?" he muttered angrily after
a few seconds.

She was beside him now, and she grabbed his arm.
"Let me help you."

Briefly he shrugged her off, and then suddenly he

went limp in the water. To Shannon's total relief, she
was able to put her hand under his chin and tow him,
with some effort, to the shallow, lapping waves.
Supporting his body against hers, her arm around his
back, gasping for breath, she staggered with him to
the sandy shore. Cold and exhausted, she dropped
down limply. She had done it! She had saved him!
The sea hadn't been able to defeat her twice. Lying
down on her back, she tried to catch her breath as
her chest heaved from exertion.

She was totally unprepared to feel Roman's
weight press down on her body as his face hovered
above hers. His hands gripped her shoulders, and his
lips took possession of hers in a savage kiss. She was
too weak to fight him, and to her horror, she found
every nerve in her shivering body responding to him
as she tried to control her breathing. His mouth
caressed hers for a long passionate moment. She was
devastatingly aware of his hard wet muscles moving
against her, heating her skin to a scorching tempera-
ture. She forgot all about the cold and the beach and
couldn't keep her arms from wrapping around his
broad back as her senses danced at his touch.

Abruptly he pulled away from her, disentangling
her arms as he stood up. "I had no intention of doing
anything more than working off my anger, Miss
Andrews, but thanks for the rescue. It was . . .
exciting. I won't forget it, I assure you."

He turned away, disappearing across the sand
toward the house.

Shivering violently, her breath coming in ragged
spurts, Shannon rolled over on the sand and cursed
bitterly. What a fool she had made of herself!

Suddenly freezing in the clinging shirt and panties,
she managed to struggle up from the sand and
brushed herself off a bit. Yanking up her slacks en
route, she rushed to her rooms.

After she had grabbed a robe from her bedroom, she ran to the shower. Beneath the hot streams of water, she tried to scrub herself free of her hateful thoughts of Roman. What must he think of her after she had let him make such an idiot of her? Of course he couldn't know the terror she had of someone drowning. He knew nothing of Jarod's disappearance. Besides, after she had thrilled to his touch, clinging to him there on the sand, how could she explain about her missing fiancé? He had already questioned the existence of a fiancé, anyway; he would never believe her now. She would just have to pretend that the scene on the beach had never happened and stay out of his way in the future.

Face flaming, she returned to her room and slipped into her nightclothes. If the man had managed to insult her, humiliate her and entice her all in two days, what would happen with him in her home for two months?

Chapter Three

Shannon had just eaten the last bite of her scrambled eggs when she heard a knock. Glancing at the clock, she saw that it was barely eight. She didn't usually have callers so early. "Oh, no," she murmured aloud, "I hope it isn't Roman Morgan." She walked reluctantly to the front door, opening it to a tall, good-looking woman.

"Excuse me," the woman said, her voice attractively tinged with a foreign accent, "but can you tell me which apartment is Roman Morgan's?"

Another woman! Shannon thought irritably. She almost couldn't believe it. Barely able to contain her hostility, she muttered, "He's upstairs to the right."

"Thank you." Shannon watched the woman's progress until she was almost to the second floor. Would the line of women never end? It was so early in the morning, and already they were knocking on his door. And each woman seemed to be more attractive than the last! Couldn't that man be satisfied with one? She heard a soft tapping. The woman responded cheerfully to Roman's warm greeting, and Shannon listened until the door was closed.

Already annoyed with him, Shannon suddenly found herself furious at his conduct. Of course she wouldn't have rented to him if she had known that he intended to use the room as a . . . a brothel! She could just barely hear the two of them talking above her, and their voices served to further anger her.

Shannon vowed that she would have a few words with Roman Morgan when his guest left. She didn't have to, and wouldn't, put up with that sort of thing!

She attempted to do some typing, but she was too angry. Fidgeting, going from one chore to another until she thought she would go crazy, she managed to get through the morning. She heard the mantel clock chime eleven, and she paused, laying aside the manuscript papers she was typing to listen for voices upstairs. She could tell that the woman was still in Roman's apartment, but even so, she decided that she might as well get the confrontation over with so that she could get it off her mind. After all, this was her home!

Her spine stiffened for the task ahead, her head held regally, she marched determinedly up the stairs, mentally practicing her speech before she knocked. Roman opened the door wide for her, and she gasped in surprise, a hand flying to her throat as she stared inside. She was unable to miss seeing the pretty woman perched on a tall stool behind Roman. And she was absolutely nude expect for a thin strip of velvet across her lap! Beautifully endowed, she showed no embarrassment at being caught naked in a man's rooms. Shannon's distress was enough for both of them. Her voice was caught somewhere in her throat, and she had to struggle to find the words.

"Well?" Roman prompted, his face showing his impatience, his arms crossed.

"You . . . you . . . what do you think you're doing?" she sputtered at last. "What do you think you're using this house for?" Seeing the woman eyeing her interestedly, Shannon gulped and stepped out of her line of vision. "How dare you . . . how dare you . . ."

Roman's deep sigh was one of displeasure. "How dare I what, Miss Andrews?"

Leaning nearer to him, she hissed, "How dare you try to turn this house into a brothel!"

His laugh was short and derisive as he shook his head in disgust. "Come inside, Miss Andrews," he ordered. Before she could escape, he had grabbed her and pulled her in.

Cheeks flaming, lips pressed tightly together, Shannon stood before the unclothed woman.

"Miss Andrews, meet Miss Lena Lanet," Roman said, still holding on to Shannon's arm. "Miss Lanet is a nude model, Miss Andrews. She poses for some of the best artists in the country, and she commands one of the largest hourly fees." He released Shannon and stood stroking his chin as he pretended to study her face. "I believe you owe Miss Lanet an apology for your uncalled-for, and unduly rash, statement."

Shannon's mouth gaped open in disbelief. She couldn't bear to look at the woman, and her glance shot to the canvas Roman had been working on. A large, provocative painting of Lena was half-finished. Acutely embarrassed, Shannon searched her wildly churning thoughts for some words to soften her accusation.

Forcing herself to look at the other woman, she murmured, "How do you do, Miss Lanet?"

"Miss Andrews." Miss Lanet tipped her head, amusement beneath her words, her gorgeous features barely suppressing a smile.

"The apology, Miss Andrews," Roman reminded her. "After all, you did imply that Miss Lanet was—"

"All right, Mr. Morgan!" Shannon exclaimed, interrupting him as she glared into his eyes. Blood pounding against her temples, fists clenched in silent fury, she turned to the woman. "I apologize," she whispered, her voice strained. "However, if you saw the number of—"

"That's sufficient," Roman snapped impatiently, speaking to her as if she were an unruly child being made to mind her manners. "Was there anything else? Your foolish errand is costing me money."

Her bitter green eyes shifted to his taunting gray ones. He was deliberately making her look like the biggest of fools. "There was nothing else. I won't keep you from your work. Good day." Using all of her willpower, she held her head high and forced herself to display some degree of composure as she walked out, her legs trembling. When she closed the door, she was sure she heard muffled laughter behind it. How could she have been so stupid? She knew Roman Morgan was a painter, and he had asked her if Jarod did portraits. She just hadn't guessed that Roman himself was a portrait painter.

She gave a startled gasp as Shirle stepped out of her rooms with a cheery "Good morning."

For once Shannon wished that Shirle was in one of her temperamental moods and not talking. She averted her eyes and murmured, "Good morning, Shirle." She reached quickly for her doorknob, but Shirle was not to be ignored this morning.

"How's the typing going on that last manuscript?" she asked, smiling.

Plastering a smile on her face, Shannon turned to Shirle. "I'm working on it."

Shirle's big brown eyes immediately searched the girl's face. "Hey, what's wrong? You look as though you lost your last friend."

"It's nothing," Shannon lied.

Shirle shook her head knowingly. "It's the new roomer, isn't it?"

At Shannon's shocked expression, she added, "Of course having a man around the house is going to bring up the old pain and heartache over Jarod. Honey, you're going to have to put him out of your mind. It's been a year. I know it's painful, but he's gone. I don't want to sound cruel, but you need to get to know other men." Putting a hand on Shannon's arm, she coaxed, "Come into my place and let me get you a cup of coffee. I think you could use one."

Smiling with more warmth than she felt, Shannon followed Shirle into the front room, but she was shocked to realize that the very last thing she had been thinking of was the first thing Shirle suspected. Shannon hadn't been thinking of Jarod at all. Blast that Roman Morgan! He had made a fool of her again. He seemed to be making a career of it, and she found it utterly intolerable. But then, he couldn't make a fool of her if she didn't let him, could he?

She allowed Shirle to lead her into the small, homey kitchen and she watched as the older woman poured two cups of coffee from a battered pot. Shannon knew that Shirle earned good money from her writing, and she never ceased to be astonished when she entered the writer's apartment. Her possessions were few and well-used and there was no sign of organization anywhere. Shannon always wondered how such a disorderly person could arrange words so skillfully.

After putting cream and sugar into Shannon's cup, Shirle handed it to her. "Well, now," she said with a bright smile, "let's talk about something pleasant, like your new roomer."

Shannon watched the cup rattle against the saucer. She quickly set it down on the table, being careful not to spill the hot, dark liquid on any of the papers stacked there.

"He's quite a handsome devil, isn't he?" Shirle continued. "What do you know about him?"

Roman Morgan was the very last person Shannon

wanted to talk about, but apparently he had captured the interest of both of her other housemates, and she had no choice. "He's . . . he's a painter, an artist from Monterey. He's only going to be with us for two months, I'm happy to say." She could have bitten her tongue. She hadn't meant to let Shirle know how she felt about him, but it had slipped out.

"Why on earth would you be happy about that?" Shirle asked, frowning. She put a ringed hand to her hair and toyed with a curl. "I should think you'd want a steady renter, and especially one as good-looking as he is." Her laugh was throaty. "Personally, I think it's great to have a man around the house."

"I don't think his painting is very successful," Shannon replied a little spitefully. "I doubt that he can afford the rent in the summer season." She didn't add that apparently he *was* able to pay for expensive models. It had been obvious that he was concerned about wasting his money when Shannon interrupted them. He had probably saved all year to be able to afford the model.

Shirle grinned as she sat down across from Shannon and shoved some papers out of the way to make room for her coffeecup. "Well, if that's the case, tell him that he can room with me—free."

At the surprised expression on Shannon's face, she laughed openly, and for a moment her brown eyes twinkled mischievously. "Don't look so shocked, my innocent," she said, shaking her red curls. "I'm only teasing, not that I think it would be a bad idea, mind you," she added. "Women do have male roommates these days, you know. He'd definitely take the chill out of a girl's bed."

Studying Shirle's attractive face, Shannon tried to think of something to say. She wondered if the writer could really be interested in Roman. Shirle was more his age; she must be in her late twenties, and Roman was at least thirty. And Shirle was certainly more sophisticated and worldly wise than she was, Shannon mused as she looked at Shirle's dark eyes fringed by auburn lashes. Shirle was tall and shapely—just the way Roman seemed to like his women. Shannon knew Shirle wasn't saving herself for any wedding. It had been too late for that a long time ago.

"I've no doubt that he could warm a woman's bed," she finally replied tartly, failing to mention that he had already been in hers, regardless of how that had come about. "He's been here three days, and he's already had three different women up there in his apartment."

Shirle's thick brows rose and she pulled a wry face. "You don't say," she remarked. "My, my, but he's a busy one."

Shannon deliberately avoided telling Shirle that at least one of the girls was, if she was to believe Roman and the woman, his model. Eager to dismiss the subject, she said, "I should have your book finished in a couple of days. The typing isn't going as well as usual, so I'd better get back to it."

"Fine," Shirle said, standing up to walk with Shannon to the door. "As long as I get it to my agent by the end of the week, I'll be happy. Say, it's pretty warm today. I'm going to lie on the beach and soak up some sun this afternoon. Interested?"

"Sure," Shannon replied brightly. "Sounds like just what I need. I'll meet you on the beach."

"Okay. See you about two o'clock."

Shannon returned to her apartment and sat down before the typewriter again. She would have to rush if she was going to finish the manuscript in two days, since she still had over a hundred pages left to type. She groaned when a heavy knock sounded on her door, having just resigned herself to a couple of hours of steady typing.

When she opened the door, she found Roman leaning against the frame, arms crossed, a smirk on his face. "Shannon," he asked quietly, "may I come in?"

"What for?" she snapped. The fewer encounters she had with him, the better.

"For one thing, I'd like to use your phone. I won't have service until the first part of next week. For another, I want to apologize if I've upset you by painting nude women in my apartment. Of course, when I told you I was a painter and you didn't seem to object, I didn't realize that you would want to limit my subjects."

Shannon took a deep breath and slowly expelled it. "I don't want to limit your subjects, Roman," she said crisply, aware of a tension in her stomach. "I . . . I just didn't realize that you were . . . that you were painting the line of women who come and go from your door."

His lips twisted into a smile. "I see. You thought that I had them in and out of my bed, didn't you?"

Shannon blushed at his bluntness. Did he have to laugh at her, even if that *was* what she had thought? Didn't he have any sense of decency? "Yes," she snapped, meeting his penetrating gaze. She averted her eyes as she saw the amusement rise in his. "Is that all you wanted to say to me?" she asked, ready to shut the door in his face.

When he smiled at her again, she tried to close the door, but he stopped it by moving his foot forward. "I asked if I could use your phone," he reminded her, his eyes mocking.

She sighed in exasperation as she opened the door for him. "Of course. It's on the desk." Stepping aside for him to enter, she watched in irritation as he

walked to the typewriter and boldly read the first line
of the page inserted there. Repeating it aloud, he
said, "'China struggled violently as the knotted
nylon tightened around the slender column of her
throat.'" His eyes met Shannon's. "Really, Shannon, you shock me. Such brutal prose. I never would
have suspected you of composing such material. Had
I guessed you were a writer, I would have suspected
you of writing romances. I mean, anyone who
rescues a disgruntled lover from the ocean doesn't
seem the type to kill off women."

A faint pink blush flooded her cheeks as she
recalled the way she had dragged him from the black
ocean waters. "I'm not a writer," she denied hotly.
"And it's terribly rude of you to read someone else's
papers."

He bowed exaggeratedly. "Do pardon me. So
you're a closet writer. Is that it?" His eyes returned
to the typed page. "You shouldn't be ashamed of it.
It sounds quite interesting."

"I didn't write it, Mr. Morgan," she declared
emphatically. "My downstairs tenant, Shirle Wayne,
is the writer. I'm merely the typist. Will you please
use the phone and leave?"

Turning to face her, Roman leaned back against
the desk and permitted his eyes to scan her slender
form. "Will you pose for me?"

She shifted uncomfortably under his scrutiny.
"I . . . I beg your pardon," she almost whispered,
unsure that she had heard what she thought she had
heard. "Did you say pose for you?"

"I did." With amusement creasing his cheeks, he
watched her expression. "It's quite legitimate, I
assure you. And you have very good lines, and
rather a haunting quality to your eyes. It hints at
suffering, which I'd be willing to bet you've never
endured. I'll pay you well."

"You surely don't mean that you want me to pose nude?" she questioned, eyes wide and incredulous.

"I surely do."

"But I don't know anything about posing! And if I did, I wouldn't pose for you! And I wouldn't pose nude for anyone! You must be out of your mind!" Involuntarily she folded her arms protectively across her chest, her eyes flashing as she stared at him.

"No one has accused me of that recently," he replied calmly with a smile. "Don't tell me you're prudish along with your other, ah, attributes, Shannon. The nude form is beautiful. Don't you agree? *You're* certainly beautiful. I'd like to see all of you."

"Well, you're not going to!" she snapped indignantly. "And if you think you're flattering me, you're wrong. I've never been more insulted in my life! I don't know what kind of person you think I am, but I'm beginning to grow concerned about you. You . . . you sound like some kind of voyeur! Just how successful is your work? Is this the only way you can find to look at naked women?"

The teasing look that had played across his face vanished under a mask of stone. Swiftly turning his back to her, he picked up the phone and dialed brusquely.

From his rigid posture, Shannon could tell that she had said way too much. He looked angry enough to throttle her, but she told herself that he deserved what she had said. Who did he think he was, strolling into her room and telling her he wanted her to undress for him? Cheeks burning, she marched toward the kitchen. She wanted to put as much distance between them as possible, and she certainly didn't want to be in the position of listening in on any more of his conversations. She had heard enough from him to last her a lifetime. After filling a kettle with water and setting it on the stove, she dropped disconsolately in a chair. She wished she'd never laid eyes on Roman Morgan. Her life hadn't been the same since.

Just when she had decided to hide in the kitchen until he had gone, she heard a knock on the door. Wearily she dragged herself from the chair, moving quickly past Roman. It looked like one of those days when she wasn't going to have a moment to herself.

Surprised to see Sam Harvard, the detective, standing before her, she cried, "Sam! Did you find Jarod? Come in."

Ushering him toward the couch, she felt a mounting excitement. Her arm linked with his, she brushed past Roman. She was aware of his hard eyes on them as he turned to stare rudely at her visitor, all the while continuing to talk on the phone.

Sam stretched his long legs before him, hunched his shoulders, and settled down on the couch. Shannon watched him eagerly, not letting his weary features dampen her anticipation. Sam's eyes skimmed suspiciously over Roman before he spoke in a low voice. "Now, I don't want you to get your hopes up too much, but I've had word that a man answering Jarod's description was recently seen in Mexico. I can't reveal the contact's name because the man is on the lam himself, but he's regarded as trustworthy in matters like this. It's been a crooked trail, but it looks like we may finally be onto something."

Unable to control her emotions, Shannon lifted her hands to her mouth to muffle a sob. Tears immediately filled her eyes and slipped down her face. "Do you mean you think Jarod is really alive?" she whispered. She could hear her heart pounding. This was the news she had prayed for. It seemed too wonderful to be true.

"It's beginning to look that way. If the man isn't Jarod, he's a dead ringer for him."

"Oh, Jarod," she breathed, laying her head back on the couch and closing her eyes. She placed the back of her hand across her eyes to hide her tears. Her voice shook when she spoke again. "I never, never believed that Jarod was dead, but it's been so long." Her eyes fluttered open and she sat up quickly. "Oh, when can I go to him, Sam? Is he well? Why is he in Mexico?"

Sam's bushy brows furrowed as he looked at the girl's feverish face. "Now, take it easy, Shannon. Nothing's positive at this point, and I don't have any answers for you. I've circulated Jarod's picture and his description everywhere and anywhere I thought it might pay off, and I've offered rewards to anyone with any information. One notice seems to have gotten some attention. That's all, so far. It gets even more complicated from here on out. The way things look, the man who fits Jarod's description has no intention of being found. To be frank with you, it begins to look like the whole drowning may have been staged. I can't say anything definitely, but it's just possible that Jarod took the money and intends to wait out the statute of limitations in hiding. You know he and Waller lifted quite a bundle from the bank."

Shannon felt her stomach tighten. Her hands twisted around each other, and she sent Sam a scathing look. "I don't believe a word of it! If he really is Jarod, and if he *is* in hiding, I'm sure he has some perfectly legitimate explanation. He was set up by Waller; I'm positive of it."

Sam shrugged apologetically. "I'm afraid only Jarod knows the truth about that, Shannon. I read the cards just as they look. I told you, I'm guessing about all this. However, experience tells me something isn't right here." He took her hand in his. "I must ask you to make every attempt to be realistic about all this. Consider all the possibilities. Leave your mind open to anything, and I do mean anything. If you don't, you may be in for a very rude awakening. A lot of questions need to be answered here, and the answers may not be pretty. If the man is Jarod, a lot of people will want to know why he's hiding out in Mexico. Now, I respect your loyalty to him, and I understand how emotionally involved you are, but I'm asking you not to be blind about him."

"You don't know for sure that he is in hiding," she countered, immediately coming to Jarod's defense. "And anything is possible. Maybe Jarod's confused about the whole thing. Maybe he had no way to return to the States. Maybe he's being held." She breathed deeply, aware that her imagination was running wild, but she couldn't help it. "Oh, it's enough that he may be alive," she cried. "It's too wonderful to believe. I can't thank you enough for all your work. What do we do from here? Can I go to him?"

Shannon wasn't even aware that Roman had walked over to them until Sam's eyes shifted to the man, measuring each feature. Shannon had completely forgotten about him. Staring up into his cold eyes, she asked, "What do you want?"

"To thank you for the use of the phone," he said coldly.

"You're welcome," she retorted tartly. She couldn't help but wonder how much of her conversation he had heard, but she was too elated to care. "Good-bye," she said, dismissing him as she looked back at Sam.

Roman turned on his heel and stalked away, banging the door loudly after him.

"When can I see Jarod?" Shannon asked again, excitement making her voice high.

Sam patted her hand. "It just isn't that easy. I'm trying to tell you that even if the man is Jarod, he doesn't want to be found. And when a man doesn't want to be found, he can be very slippery. It will cost a lot of money to pay off my connections if we're to catch him before he runs."

Shannon blinked her green eyes at him. "But how would he know we were coming? If you know where he is, why can't we just go there?"

Releasing her hand, Sam stroked his jaw. "I don't think you're listening to me. The man who fits Jarod's description doesn't want to be found—by anyone. He's living with a . . . an individual in a little house in a squalid section of a small village. He's grown a beard and he's put on weight in an effort to disguise himself. He hardly ever leaves the house. It would be impossible to approach him without a go-between. This isn't a game, Shannon. If this man is Jarod, he'll run at the first sign of anyone."

Shannon's lower lip slipped between her teeth and she bit down on it. "Jarod won't run from me," she murmured. "I know he won't. Oh, Sam, set it up so that I can go to him."

He studied her misty green eyes. "There's an additional large sum of money involved, Shannon. We have to pay our contact to keep an eye on the man until we can get to him."

Shannon experienced a sudden letdown. She was running out of money. Sam had already requested a goodly sum for the last contact, and his own weekly fee was a large one. Her green eyes darkened. "How much money?"

He looked at her steadily. "Five hundred for the contact. If the man is Jarod, the reward of a thousand has to be paid, and you have to finance the trip. It may mean staying in a motel for at least a day or two while things are set up, or if we have to follow the man.''

She fought her rising tears. "It's a lot of money for me," she murmured, "but I'll get it somewhere. Just let me work on it a couple of days; I'll find it somehow.''

Looking at her sympathetically, he nodded and stood up to leave. "Don't take too long, Shannon. If he suspects anything, or just gets nervous, he'll bolt again. He's a sharp one. This is the first real sign we've seen of him all year. Try to get the money in a few days if you want me to close in on him.''

She stood up and escorted him to the door, but she was so distracted that she didn't even hear his good-bye. Over two thousand dollars in addition to Sam's weekly fee! How would she get it? She had already depleted her savings. She would get only about four hundred dollars from Shirle when she finished the manuscript. Sam wanted the money in a few days, and she had already spent the rent money on the household expenses and the second mort- gage on the house. What was she going to do? Collapsing on the couch, Shannon placed her fingers to her temples. She would try to get a bank loan or maybe a third mortgage on the house. She grabbed her purse and car keys and rushed out the door.

The trip proved futile and she drove home in a daze. She had to think of something. She had to! The money she earned from the rent went for utilities and other expenses, including a car pay- ment. If she sold her car, she would have no way to travel, and in Southern California it was almost impossible to get around without a car. She entered her apartment and sat down to think and became so lost in her problems that she almost forgot that she was supposed to meet Shirle. She really had more important things to do.

Sighing wearily, she stood up. The beach was as good as any place to think, and it was a beautiful day. The sun would be warm and maybe she would relax. Besides, she had already told Shirle she would meet her, and she prided herself on keeping her word. Lying on the beach and engaging in idle chatter might even perk her up. Hastily slipping off her clothes and changing into a brief orange bikini, she grabbed an oversized towel and hurried out.

"Over here," Shirle called from where she had settled herself on a spot directly in front of the house. Shannon quickly spread her towel and lay down.

"Don't look now," Shirle murmured, arching her back and staring out to sea, "but we have an admirer."

"Where?" Shannon asked, controlling an impulse to look around.

"From our very own balcony."

Shannon turned and glared at the house. Just as she expected, Roman was watching them. "Oh, him," she retorted sharply, quickly turning back around.

"Yes, him," Shirle breathed, boldly staring up at Roman as he rested his elbows on the rail of his balcony, looking in their direction. Shirle finally dragged her eyes back to Shannon. "He can watch me all day if he wants to." She laughed suggestively. "He can do more than watch, if he's interested."

"You'd better watch out for him," Shannon declared. "The first thing you know, he'll be asking you to pose in the nude for him."

Shirle giggled in obvious fascination. "In the nude? You must be kidding. Does he paint nudes?"

"He sure does." In lowered tones she told Shirle

about the scene she had walked in on just that morning.

Shirle laughed. "So that's why you were so upset when you came down this morning. You should have told me. I had no idea it was that man who'd upset you. It's a charming story. Now, let me see," she said, watching the ocean waves, "what kind of mystery story could I get out of that? I've got it! Handsome painter lures models to his room with the promise of fame and big money, and when they have their defenses down, so to speak, he stabs them to death with the sharp end of a paintbrush."

"Shirle!" Shannon protested. "How perfectly gruesome."

Shirle laughed again. "Gruesome for you, but business as usual for me. He would make an excellent character. Hmmm, maybe it would be nice if he did want me to pose for him. Purely as research," she added with a smile. "Think of the things I could learn about him."

"Shirle, you wouldn't!" Shannon cried. "And I wouldn't put it past him. He already asked *me* to pose for him. I couldn't believe his nerve!"

Shirle rolled over on her stomach, propped up on her elbows and twisted her head to stare at Shannon with new interest. "Lucky you! What did you say?"

"I refused, of course!" Shannon declared with indignation. "And then he tried to entice me with the promise of money. Really, he's terrible. I'm sorry I rented to him, but I don't have any legitimate excuse to force him out."

"Don't you dare get rid of him," Shirle insisted. Then her voice lowered suddenly. "And don't run him off now. He's coming toward us."

Shannon sat up just as Roman stopped in front of her. Glaring at him through narrowed lids, she willed him to go away, but he boldly permitted his eyes to look at every inch of her.

"Are you the downstairs tenant?" he asked, looking at Shirle when he had finished his insolent perusal of Shannon.

With a broad smile, Shirle sat up. "I certainly am. Shirle Wayne," she said, extending a hand.

"Roman Morgan." He clasped her hand warmly and gave her such an engaging smile that Shannon decided it had to be phony. "Your phone is ringing incessantly, Miss Wayne. I thought you might like to know in case it's important. Someone seems rather persistent."

Looking at Roman with openly admiring eyes, Shirle hopped up. "Call me Shirle, Roman. Thanks for telling me about the phone. It's probably my agent. Catch you later." She yanked up her towel and scampered away, leaving Shannon to face Roman.

"You're blocking my sun," she said in a tight little voice. "Kindly move." Her eyes swept over him before she could control their movement, taking in the wavy hair, challenging eyes, and arrogant, attractive body. Standing there much too close, dressed in a navy tank top that made no pretense of covering the broad chest and well-defined shoulders, and pale blue shorts which molded his lean hips and emphasized his long, muscular legs, Roman Morgan was all male, from the top of his dark head all the way down to his high-arched feet.

"I beg your pardon," he replied sarcastically. "It's really a shame, Shannon, that you aren't as pleasant as you look. When you change your mind about modeling for me, let me know. Of course, maybe you're so well-to-do that even the money wouldn't tempt you. I'd be willing to pay you a hundred dollars an hour. Most people are impressed by that amount."

Shannon's mouth opened and she was about to scream that she didn't care how much the fee was, but Roman stalked away before she had the chance. She lay back down on her towel, closed her eyes and sighed. Why did he bring out the very worst in her? And where on earth did he get a hundred dollars an hour to pay a nude model? It was a tidy sum. That girl who modeled for him this morning must have stayed for at least four hours. Four hundred dollars for a morning of posing! It was staggering!

Why, if a girl worked regularly, she could earn . . . Shannon stopped figuring, astonished at what she was thinking. If she posed for Roman, she could earn two thousand dollars in a week. Of course, that was probably the fee only the top models earned. She didn't imagine they worked regularly very often. Her thoughts caused her to blush. Not even for Jarod would she pose nude! And she certainly didn't want her body and face on canvas for all the world to see.

But where would she get the money? Sam had said that he wanted it in a few days. Shannon felt the tears forming in her eyes. After all this time, she had at last found some reason to think that Jarod might be alive. She had to go and see for herself. If she didn't, she couldn't live with herself. She had to get that money some way. Any way. Too restless to remain on the beach with such thoughts eating at her, Shannon picked up the towel and slowly walked toward the house.

She was surprised to see Roman sitting out on the main patio, watching her. His legs were wide apart, his hands thrust down in his pockets, and he was leaning back in the chair in a posture Shannon considered intimidatingly masculine. But then, she conceded, Roman was intimidatingly masculine in any posture. His eyes burned holes in her as his bold gaze roved over her. Trying to look anywhere but at him, Shannon hurried across the sand, stepped through the gateless picket fence, and walked onto the bricks. She heard a car door slam in the alley, but she paid no attention to it. Suddenly Roman stood up and strode toward her. Hastening her steps, she tried to reach her apartment before he caught up with her. She didn't want to hear any more of his propositions. She was so desperate for money that she might be tempted to give in to him!

Before she could escape him, he stepped up beside her. Grabbing her by the arms, he crushed her to his hard chest as he covered her mouth with a passionate kiss. Her hands, still holding the beach towel, were pressed against his body in such a way that she couldn't even fight. She opened her eyes and stared into his for just a moment. When she attempted to draw her head away, his kiss deepened, sending tiny thrills to the depth of her being. Her heart pounded wildly and the fight went out of her. Roman stirred sensations in her that she hadn't known existed. Jarod had never been able to arouse her the way this arrogant man did. His body set hers on fire. She had been warm and comfortable in Jarod's love, but this brute of a man was able to make her soul flame with his touch. She felt the towel slip from her grasp, and it fell to the patio as her arms slid around Roman's back to hold him to her. His brief shirt was a scant shield between them, and she felt her breasts tingle beneath her thin bikini top. Tracing Roman's muscles with her fingertips, she was lost in his embrace as she pressed her barely clothed body to his. She had a burning awareness of his hands moving over the naked skin of her back as she abandoned herself to his skilled seduction.

Her eyelids opened wide when she heard the tapping of the heels on the bricks and a muffled cry. "Roman!"

As Roman slowly freed her, Shannon turned to look into the tear-filled eyes of the young woman who had run from Roman's room sobbing. Her hands were pressed to her face, and Shannon couldn't miss the huge wedding set that glittered there. What if this woman was Roman's wife? She certainly seemed to think that she had every reason to be shocked by seeing him kiss another woman. In an instant Shannon had grabbed up the beach towel and fled.

Slamming her door shut, she pressed against it in disgust. She could hear Roman and the woman he had called Elleen arguing out on the brick patio. Shannon herself was still shaking from the effects of his kiss. He had made a fool of her again! And now it seemed that he was a married man! The thought of it caused her stomach to turn somersaults. She knew she had to find Jarod at any cost. She couldn't let Roman Morgan tempt her again with his physical attractions. She felt her cheeks warm as a shameful blush crept into them.

Flinging the towel on the floor, she stalked to her closet to grab a robe, all the while trying to rid herself of thoughts of Roman. Robe in hand, she rushed to her bathroom and climbed into the shower. How he must be laughing at her! She turned the taps until the water was as hot as she could stand it, and scrubbed every inch of her body, but she just couldn't cleanse her mind of Roman Morgan.

She had just returned to her room and dressed in a scarlet caftan when she heard a rap on the door. She didn't care who it was this time. She would not answer it. Her apartment had been like Grand Central Station all day long, and she was in no mood for another visitor. The knock sounded again, and she covered her ears with her hands.

"Shannon!" a male voice growled, "I know you're in there."

Walking to the front door, she stood before it with her fists balled up. "I don't want to talk to you. Go away," she called back through the closed door.

There was silence for a brief time before he responded. "I want to apologize for what happened," he said in a low voice.

"Apology not accepted," she snapped.

"Open this door," he growled. "I want to talk to you."

"No!"

"I won't leave until I've spoken to you," he insisted. "Let me in!"

"Don't give me orders in my own home, mister!" she shouted.

"Are you afraid to see me?" he taunted.

"I don't want to see you. Can't you get that through your thick head? You have enough girls hanging around without bothering me. Get away from my door. Every time I'm in your company, something goes wrong for me. Just go away! Leave me alone."

"I'm not leaving until you open this door and let me have my say," he declared.

"Go away before you disturb everyone in the house!" she muttered coldly.

Roman rapped soundly on her door again. "Shannon! Open this door!" he commanded in a loud voice.

"Oh, you . . . you savage!" she cried. She jerked the door open and glared at him. "Have your say and then leave!" she demanded hostilely. "You're determined to bother everyone in the house, aren't you?"

Before she could block his passage, he pushed his way into her apartment and closed the door. Grabbing her by the wrists, he pulled her to him. "Does that include you, Shannon? Do I bother *you?*" he murmured suggestively as he stared down into her angry eyes.

He was standing much too close to her, and she could smell the faint aroma of a musky after-shave lotion. "Let go of me!" she retorted, green eyes blazing. "Tell me what you want and get out!"

He released her wrists abruptly, but he remained standing so near to her that she could smell the maleness of him and feel the animal warmth he exuded. "I'm not sorry for that kiss outside," he drawled. "I enjoyed it thoroughly, and I could tell you did, too." His lips curved into a small smile. "However, I will apologize for putting you on the spot like that with Elleen."

"You knew she was approaching when you did it, didn't you?" she accused.

Undaunted, Roman nodded his dark head. "I did. Frankly, I was trying to discourage her."

"From what?" Shannon hissed. "Who is she that you treat her so despicably? I saw a wedding set on her hand."

Shannon was surprised to see the expression in Roman's eyes become cold and bitter. "It's a long story. One I have no intention of getting into with you. But to show you that I'm genuinely sorry to have involved you, let me take you to dinner tonight."

"That won't be necessary."

Roman stepped nearer to her, and Shannon felt her heart begin to beat erratically. "I know it isn't necessary. I want to do it. You see, I don't believe that you have a fiancé, Shannon. A woman in love with one man wouldn't respond the way you do to a kiss from another. I think you invented that tale to keep the wolves at bay. You're very pleasing to the eyes, and I'd like to get to know you better."

"Well, I wouldn't like to get to know *you* better!" she snapped. "And you're most certainly wrong about my fiancé," she announced, trying to make her tone harsh. She couldn't deny that she found his close proximity provocative. Her lips wanted nothing more than to feel his caress them again. Her arms longed to wrap around the broadness of his back. Even as angry as she was, she wanted to be pressed close to his hard chest. "I have no need to lie to you. I've been engaged for two years."

"Taking his time, isn't he?" Roman taunted, arching an eyebrow. "I wouldn't leave a warm little thing like you toasting on the burner for two years. I hope your fiancé isn't that man who was here this morning."

His reference to Sam Harvard annoyed her even more. Her voice was icy when she spoke. "He is not. Who my fiancé is is none of your business. My story, like yours, Mr. Morgan, is a long and involved one. One *I* have no intention of sharing with *you!*"

His lips parted in a half-smile. "Fine. All I want from you is your company at dinner tonight. Let me make up for that little scene on the patio."

"No, thank you."

His eyes searched hers, and she was surprised to hear him say, "Please."

She wanted to refuse. He was rude and impossible and arrogant. She wanted to tell him to have dinner with one of his string of girls, but she heard herself telling him to call for her at six. He nodded and left.

In a cloud of confusion, she dropped down on the couch. Why was she having anything to do with him? Everything went all wrong for her when he was around. And her heart belonged to Jarod, though she was shocked by the feelings Roman aroused in her. She had never loved anyone but Jarod. She never would love anyone but Jarod. But she was only too aware that she had never felt in Jarod's arms the way she felt in Roman's. It was confusing and frightening. She could only attribute it to the strain she had been under this past year. If only the man in Mexico was Jarod. She was sure everything would be all right then. She had only to be held in Jarod's arms once more to have her world set straight. No matter what Jarod's reasons for his disappearance, she was sure things could be worked out. She loved Jarod with all her heart, and she knew that that love would see them through anything.

So why was she looking forward to the dinner with Roman with such anticipation?

Chapter Four

Pondering over what to wear, Shannon finally selected a pale blue gown made of a shimmering material. She hadn't worn it since the engagement party the bank employees had given for her and Jarod two years ago. Jarod had loved the gown and she knew she looked especially pretty in it. Feeling a bit guilty about wearing her best gown for Roman Morgan, she slipped her feet into matching blue high heels and studied her reflection in the mirror.

She hadn't thought to ask Roman where they would be dining, but she decided that a man who paid a model a hundred dollars an hour couldn't be as poor as she had first suspected. He might prefer one of the elegant restaurants along the beach or on the bay. Smoothing the form-fitting gown over her hips, she adjusted the slightly plunging neckline. The gown showed off her shapely figure to perfection, and the long sleeves would ward off the night chill. Picking up a brush from her vanity, she stroked her hair until it shone with brilliant highlights, then decided to put it up on her head. After plaiting it into one long braid, she coiled it gracefully around her head and stood back to admire her work. The style accented her eyes and cheekbones and she liked the effect. She applied a dark lipstick and painted her eyelids a pale blue. The color made her enchanting eyes look more blue than green and she was pleased with her appearance when she finished dressing.

When Roman appeared promptly at six, Shannon had just finished putting on her makeup. Feeling a little breathless, she hurried to the door. She was glad she had dressed so carefully for the occasion when she saw Roman standing before her in a white dinner jacket and dark maroon trousers. A deep plum shirt set off his dramatic good looks, and Shannon felt her pulse race at the sight of him. Her decision to dress in her prettiest gown had been the right one for a change, and she hoped the rest of the evening would go as well.

Somehow Roman had secured dinner reservations at one of the area's most exclusive restaurants. Names were usually taken weeks in advance, and Shannon marveled that they were ushered right in. She was sure the maître d' acted as if he knew Roman, and she was surprised when they were led to a table overlooking the bay. Shannon smiled as she looked out at the calm waters, the lighted yachts and the small boats. For just this once, it would be wonderful to forget about the scandal of Jarod's alleged crime and subsequent disappearance, her heartache and her desperate need for money with which to find him. Again Roman's request for her to pose nude for him rushed to mind. She decided firmly that even love wouldn't induce her to go to such lengths.

"Shall we start with wine?" he asked, touching her hand lightly as he broke into her thoughts. She couldn't help but be aware of his dark good looks and his charm as she sat across from him. "I assume you do drink."

"Yes," she confessed, smiling at him. "And I'd love some wine."

"Good." He motioned to the waiter and soon they were served tall glasses of white wine.

When the waiter returned to ask if they were ready to order, Roman looked at her questioningly. "Ready?"

She had been so engrossed in her thoughts that she hadn't taken time to read the menu. "Yes. You order for me," she suggested. "I feel like a surprise tonight."

He laughed deeply, his gray eyes twinkling with amusement. "You may just get one," he said in a teasing tone.

After he had ordered, Roman entertained her with impersonal accounts of the painting world and his life in Monterey. She had to admit that she had never been to his city, and he pretended shock, pointing out the beauty of the area. She noted that he was careful not to include any serious information about himself or his family as he talked, but she didn't mind. She didn't want to touch on any deep or painful subjects herself, and she found the light conversation very soothing. She was pleased with the meal Roman ordered for her, and she didn't even notice when he edged a little closer to her, his arm lightly brushing hers as he laughed with her over some silly remark she had made. He was radiating charm and Shannon was happy that she had consented to go out with him. He made her feel beautiful and special, and she could understand why he had a line of women at his door.

Even as she thought about his women, she experienced an uneasy sensation. Not wanting to believe it, she thought she heard the ominous tapping of heels. She clutched her wineglass tightly in her hand, unwilling to drag her eyes from Roman's face.

"So! You really are here," a bitter female voice

spoke accusingly, forcing Shannon to look up to see
Elleen standing by their table, her pretty face distorted with anger. "May I sit down?" she hissed.

"You may not," Roman responded coldly. "Go
away."

As though his disdain had the power to cause the
blonde to vanish, he turned back to Shannon nonchalantly. "Now, let's see. What were you saying?"
Totally ignoring the other woman, who stood rigidly
by the table with tears in her blue eyes, Roman gave
Shannon his undivided attention.

Elleen reached out and touched his arm. Immediately he shrugged her hand away. "Please, Roman,"
she pleaded in a low, softened voice. Shannon
couldn't keep herself from staring at the woman. She
was touched by the shimmering of tears in her
pained eyes. Elleen raised a hand to her long blond
hair, brushing a strand away from her face with
slightly shaking fingers. "I must talk to you,
Roman."

Embarrassed, Shannon looked nervously around
the room. She knew that they were attracting a
number of amused stares and quick, barely concealed glances of curiosity. Roman noticed too, and
he jabbed a finger at the empty chair beside him. His
voice was angry as he muttered, "Say whatever it is
you seem bound to say and stop chasing me around.
What does it take to make you understand that there
is nothing left between us? Can't you see that I have
more interesting things to do?" he demanded.

Shannon sucked in her breath at his ruthlessness.
She could see no excuse for his behavior. Was this
the same charming companion with whom she had
just shared dinner?

With a haughty show of grace, Elleen seated
herself by Roman and turned her hate-filled eyes
toward Shannon. "Who is she, Roman?" she asked

bitterly. "I know you don't love her. You can't. Not after what we've meant to each other. Is she your new model? Why are you torturing me like this?" She turned back to him, tears glistening in her eyes. "Only love would drive me to humiliate myself like this."

For the briefest of seconds Shannon thought she saw a softening of the hard line of Roman's jaw, but she decided she must have imagined it. Disgust was evident on his face as he clenched his teeth and laced his fingers together. "No one asked you to humiliate yourself. I didn't put you in the position of following me around. I don't want you here. How strongly do I need to impress that fact on you? It's over between us. I don't love you."

He unlaced his fingers to take Shannon's hand in his. She wanted to pull away from him, but she didn't have the courage. "I'm going to marry this delicious creature. She has honored me by consenting to become my bride." He ignored the shock on Shannon's face and turned the coldest eyes she had ever seen to Elleen. "Now, will you please go away and leave us alone?"

Shannon lowered her eyes, ashamed to look at the other woman. When she heard the sob that caught in Elleen's throat, she looked to see its effect on Roman. He was staring at her with his steel-gray eyes, but they betrayed nothing.

Elleen put a hand on his arm again and said huskily, "I don't believe you." Her lips quivered with uncertainty. "You weren't in love with her two weeks ago. Who is she?"

A gloating smile appeared on Roman's lips. "Elleen Morgan—Mrs. Roman Morgan—meet my fiancée, Miss Shannon Andrews."

Shannon's head jerked toward the other woman in surprise. She had been right! A flood of words rushed to her mouth, but she was too startled to say them. Elleen was Roman's wife!

Shannon stood up abruptly, knocking over her wineglass as she did so. Roman had used her again, and this time she was thoroughly outraged!

Roman automatically released her hand to grab the glass, and Shannon used the moment to flee. She had never been so appalled in her life. She didn't care that the other diners turned to look at her. How dare he introduce her to his wife as his fiancée! He was even more loathsome than she had imagined. She didn't know what compelled that poor woman to follow him around like that. Had she no shame? Regardless, Shannon would be no part of their battle.

She rushed blindly toward the exit, holding up the hem of her gown as she ran. When she stepped out onto the sidewalk, she heard heavy footsteps behind her. She didn't dare turn to see if it was Roman. Instead, she ducked into a nearby restaurant. Unsure of what to do then, she darted into the ladies' room. For at least twenty minutes she stayed there, hidden. Once she thought she heard Roman's deep voice as he spoke to a woman outside. When the woman came into the restroom, Shannon remained quiet, and after a few minutes the woman left. Not until she felt fairly certain that the coast was clear did she hurry to a public phone and call a taxi. Then she waited inside a few minutes, giving it time to arrive.

Huddled in a corner in the backseat of the cab, she seethed with anger at Roman's behavior. He had used her to hurt his wife! What kind of man would do such a thing? On the pretext of an apology, he had set her up to humiliate that poor woman. Shannon didn't believe for a single minute that Roman hadn't staged the whole thing. Such a meeting could have been no coincidence. He had probably phoned Elleen and told her he would be there. His actions were inexcusable and she never wanted to see him again.

When the taxi stopped in front of Blue Haven, she paid the driver and ran to her apartment. She wasn't really surprised to find Roman waiting for her, but she shoved past him to insert the key. When it triggered the lock, she flung the door open and marched inside, flipping a light switch as she entered.

Roman followed close behind her.

Whirling around to face him, she threatened in a low hissing voice, "Get out of here or I'll scream my head off. Shirle and Mrs. Angel will call the police at the first sound."

With incredible speed Roman closed the door with one hand and fastened the other over Shannon's mouth, flattening her against the wall. "You'll do no such thing. You will listen quietly to what I have to say, or I'll keep you in this position until you do."

Shannon tried to strike him, but he skillfully captured both her hands in one of his. Enraged, helpless, tears rising to her eyes, she had no choice but to hear him out. In this position, she couldn't even curse his vile behavior. Glaring at him with all the hate she had in her, she nodded, and he released her.

Grasping her hand, he dragged her to the couch, shoved her down and dropped down beside her. "I am well aware that I owe you an explanation. If you'll be quiet long enough, you'll get it. I'm in no mood to listen to another woman's fury, so just this one time, don't interrupt me."

"First tell me one thing," Shannon demanded, determined not to listen until she heard the answer.

Roman leaned over dangerously close to her. "What is it?"

"Is Elleen your wife? I mean, is she still married to you?"

His laugh was short and harsh. "She never was my wife. She's married to my father; she has been for two weeks. I'm Roman Morgan the Second." She couldn't read the expression in his eyes as he looked at her levelly. "My father is better known to his friends as Rome Morgan, owner of Pirate Morgan, Roman Dreams, and Morgan's Glory—very famous racehorses in case you aren't familiar with the racing world."

He waited for a reaction from Shannon, and he got one. Of course she knew the name. It hadn't occurred to her to associate it with Roman. Rome Morgan's horses were world-renowned.

Roman smiled harshly. "I see you know the name. Most women do once they connect it with the race world. Elleen certainly did. Until last month, she had planned to marry me."

He paused again, and Shannon didn't know what to say. She could see the coldness in his eyes, and she held her breath, waiting for the rest of his story.

"Elleen found my father fascinating, as, apparently, he found her. In the beginning he set out to prove that she was just another gold-digger. She was my favorite model, and I spent a lot of time with her. Rome bitterly opposed a marriage between us. The irony is that he married her instead. She consented to go on a trip with him, and they came home married. Unfortunately, now she seems to think that she wants both of us." His eyes searched Shannon's. "I was serious when I introduced you as my fiancée. I want you to marry me."

"You must be crazy!" she cried. "After the way

you've treated me, I wouldn't marry you if you were the last man alive!"

He laughed, but there was no mirth in the sound. "I know how that little scene in the restaurant must have looked to you, but I didn't plan it. I can only assume that Elleen came here to find me, and your friend Shirle told her where I was. I met her on the way to your door, and after she commented on my attire, I mentioned that we were going to dinner."

"Oh."

"Will you marry me?" he repeated.

Shannon shook her head, trying to make some sense of it all. "No, I won't marry you. I can't marry you," she whispered. "You don't love me."

His answer was quick and sharp. "Love doesn't enter into it. I've seen the way love makes a fool of a man. You've fabricated a fiancé. Now I'm offering you a husband."

Shannon couldn't meet his hard gaze. "You're just doing this for revenge against Elleen and your father," she murmured in a low voice.

The silence was oppressive when he failed to answer. She looked up to find his eyes searching her face. "Yes, I am," he replied. "I'll make no demands on you. If you meet a man later and want your freedom, you'll be free to go. Ours will be a paper marriage. If it should end, I'll see that you're well cared for. Right now I want the appearance of a wife."

Shannon felt pains shoot through her heart. Somehow she knew that if she ever married this man, she couldn't stand to live with him without his love. "But you can find a hundred girls to agree to that kind of marriage," she said, staring into his eyes. "Why me?"

"Circumstances," he replied tersely. "Elleen's

seen you with me a couple of times. She'll believe that it's a real marriage, and she'll be forced to face the reality of it."

In her shock and anger, Shannon had at first completely forgotten about her own pressing problems. She would never marry without love. And Jarod was the man she loved. Yet she had completely forgotten about Jarod when Roman had proposed. What on earth was the matter with her? Why was she even listening to him? She wasn't the fickle type. With her, true love meant forever with one man. And hadn't Jarod been the man she had chosen for life?

A nagging doubt crept into her mind as she sat beside Roman. Was there any truth to his insinuation that her love for Jarod was less than real if they had felt no pressing desire to marry? It had been her idea to have a long engagement; she had wanted to be sure that Jarod was ready to settle down and raise a family, but that didn't mean that she didn't love him deeply. They had even talked of converting the two bottom apartments into one so that they would have rooms for the children, but plans took time and money. Shannon hadn't wanted a hasty wedding, but was that odd? Wasn't true love more than a headlong rush into bed? And yet with Roman, all she could think about was the way she felt in his arms, the way her heart pounded at his very nearness, the way . . . She shoved these thoughts to the back of her mind. She despised him for the doubts that he was deliberately trying to create. He was taking advantage of her position and his own compelling masculinity. Well, his plan wouldn't succeed with her. Jarod was the man she loved.

"I really do have a fiancé," she stated firmly. "He was presumed drowned, but I've just received word that he may be alive in Mexico."

Puzzled, Roman frowned at her. "I don't understand."

Words tumbling over each other, Shannon told him the whole story. "All I'm waiting for now is money to go to him," she concluded.

She was appalled by the sudden anger Roman directed at her. "Don't be a little fool!" he growled. "Don't tell me you've been pining away here for a year while some petty criminal makes a patsy of you. Girl, if the man wanted you, he would have found some way to have sent for you."

Shannon flushed. "You don't understand," she said, wondering how he managed to make her feel like an idiot for trusting Jarod. "I'm sure Jarod would have sent for me if it were at all possible."

Roman sneered disgustedly. "You naive little thing. The very least he could have done was phone you to let you know he was alive."

Shannon immediately became defensive. Everyone else had turned on Jarod, but she felt the same intense loyalty for him as always. He was a dreamer, she knew, but dreamers were important to the world. His idealistic, happy-go-lucky attitude had been part of his charm. But he wasn't a criminal. Shannon would never believe that Jarod was guilty of taking that money from the bank. She knew him, and because he wasn't here to defend himself, she felt she must speak up for him.

"You don't know anything about it," she snapped. "Jarod loves me. He'll have an explanation; I'm sure of it. He does love me." Her eyes met his. "And I love him. There will never be any man for me but Jarod." She looked down to see her hands twisting in her lap, and she stopped their movement, sure that Roman would see her nervousness and the uncertainty he had created within her.

He was silent for a few minutes while he watched

her. "I see," he said finally. "In that case, pose for me and I'll see that you have your two thousand dollars in three days."

Shannon's eyes looked up to meet his, and she felt her heart jump. She didn't know what to say. She couldn't go to such drastic lengths for the money, but if she didn't, where else would she get it?

Seeing her hesitation and confusion, he snarled, "If you love this man as much as you claim you do, you would do anything for the money, and posing hardly puts a strain on you. All you do is sit there."

"Nude," she retorted bitterly, humiliated, but knowing full well that the thought of the money tempted her.

"Plenty of women would jump at the chance," he snapped.

"Then why don't you ask one of them?"

"I want you. You're fresh and beautiful and you have a natural grace. Besides, I told you already that I want to capture that look in your eyes. Most nude models are too aware of the world to affect that troubled look with any believability. I suppose you attribute it to the loss of your true love?" he added contemptuously.

Ignoring his spiteful comment, she hung her head. "I just can't. I can't . . . undress in front of you."

His laughter was cynical. "I'm not asking you to sleep with me—just to pose."

She raised her troubled eyes to his. "But I'll be caught on canvas for anyone who wants to look."

"That's right. But you'll also have money to find your . . . fiancé."

She lowered her eyes again, caught between shame and temptation. Even if she agreed, she would die of embarrassment sitting before Roman naked. "I can't," she said again.

Standing up, he turned to her. "As the old cliché

goes, everyone has a price. You think about it. If you love the man as much as you say, you'll see fit to pay the price. Let me know in the morning.''

When she looked up again, he was gone and she was alone with her thoughts. Just when she convinced herself that Roman was right—if she loved Jarod enough, she wouldn't give up this chance to find him—she changed her mind again. It was totally against her principles to pose nude for anyone. The idea was repugnant to her.

And to pose for Roman! She thought of his warm body pressed against hers, the way his kisses aroused her until she thought she couldn't stand it, the wild beating of her heart when she was near him. Her very body would betray her if she were sitting naked before him. Her face flamed with embarrassment. She couldn't pose for Roman. Stripping off the lovely gown, she flung it to the floor.

She stepped out of her lacy panties and removed her sheer bra, staring at her body in the full-length mirror. She had always known that her beauty was the kind to turn men's heads, even though she wasn't full-figured like Miss Lanet or stunning like Elleen, with her cool blond looks. Her breasts were rounded and high, her waist small, her hips curved without being broad. Her legs were slim and long and her ankles trim. She tried to imagine herself perched on the tall stool as she had last seen Miss Lanet. She backed away from the mirror. She could never do it, sitting there nonchalantly as if she were passing the time of day. Grabbing her nightclothes, she quickly covered her nakedness. She couldn't see her body on canvas in some man's bedroom.

Shannon flipped out the light and got into bed, but sleep was a long time coming. She tried to think about Jarod, to find some comfort in the familiar lines of his boyish face, but she found that Roman's handsome face invaded her mind, with its strong, dramatic, masculine features, piercing gray eyes and black wavy hair. Finally she fought the vision until she could replace it with Jarod's smiling face. She could see his crooked grin, his blond hair ruffled by a breeze, and the way he walked with a jaunty step. She could feel his arms around her, and she felt ashamed that she had enjoyed being held by Roman. Shannon was all Jarod had. If she didn't pursue his disappearance, no one would. His name would be blackened forever. Tears rose to her eyes and slipped down her cheeks. She had actually listened when Roman talked about marriage. And now she was thinking of posing for him.

But only for Jarod. Her Jarod.

When Shannon awakened the next morning, she didn't even look at her clock. Slipping quickly into jeans and a T-shirt, she walked out of her apartment and up the steps to Roman's apartment before she had a chance to think about it. She knocked twice and waited for him to answer. Dressed in his cutoffs, without shoes or shirt, his dark wavy hair tumbled, he opened the door just a bit and yawned sleepily. "What is it? What time is it?" His eyes looked dreamy with sleep. "I was sleeping."

Shannon shrugged, not knowing what time it was, and afraid to do anything besides state her purpose for being there. "I want to pose for you," she said, her voice shaky, the words rushed.

Surprise crossed his face for the briefest of seconds, and he awakened fully. She almost backed down the steps then, for she realized that he had never expected her to agree. "Fine," he said. "Come on in. I'll make coffee. You look as if you could use a cup."

She didn't know whether to stay or go. Now that

she had committed herself, she didn't want to say anything more. Taking her by the arm, he pulled her inside. "Come on."

Following him to the kitchen, she settled stiffly into one of the chairs. Watching as he poured water into an automatic coffeemaker, she saw him look at the clock on the wall.

"It's only seven," he said, turning to her with a peculiar smile. "You couldn't wait to tell me you wanted to undress for me, could you?"

She didn't understand him. He had asked her to pose. Now he seemed almost nasty about it, phrasing it so crudely. Hurt by his attitude, she stood up. "It was your idea," she said defensively. "If you've changed your mind, I'm sure it's for the best." She brushed past him, heading out of the room. "Sorry to have gotten you up."

Placing his hand firmly on her shoulder, he pushed her back down on the chair. "Take it easy." His voice was low. "I want you to pose for me. I'm pleased that you agreed."

Although his words sounded convincing, his cold eyes denied them. Shannon sighed. She pitied the poor girl who would marry this man. Besides the bitterness that he wore like a badge, he was dangerously explosive.

"Cream and sugar?" he asked.

She stared blankly at him, seeing only his broad shoulders and hairy chest, then realized what he had said and nodded.

He set a cup of coffee on the table before her. She watched him cautiously as he ran a hand over his jaw. "I would have shaved if I had known you were coming."

She looked away, embarrassed. "It doesn't matter. When do you want . . . when do you want me to pose?"

Inclining his head, he studied her critically. Then he murmured dispassionately, "Whenever. Today at nine?"

Shannon tried to force her eyes to meet his as she pretended nonchalance, but she couldn't do it. Head bowed, she nodded.

He sat down next to her and she tried to take a sip of her coffee, but her hands were trembling too much to lift the cup to her lips. Thinking about how she was about to degrade herself, she fought against rising tears. She knew men liked to look at pretty women, but she had been shy at the thought of even Jarod seeing her fully unclothed. He had often tried to persuade her to undress for him, maintaining that in a bikini she was almost naked anyway. But she didn't feel almost naked at all, and that was the difference.

"Having second thoughts?" Roman challenged, his voice sarcastic.

Shannon was annoyed that he seemed able to read her thoughts. She forced herself to look at him. "No, not at all," she lied. "I was just thinking that I sould go down and . . . and curl my hair and put on my makeup." Her laughter was brittle. "After all, I want to look my best when I make my modeling debut, don't I?"

The expression in his eyes was frigid, but he replied lightly. "Most people won't concentrate on your face when they see the painting."

Shannon could feel her face heat up, but she wouldn't turn from his gaze. "Be that as it may," she replied defiantly, ignoring her shaking knees, "I want to look good."

His lips curved into a smile. "I've no doubt that you will."

Trying to conceal her nervousness, she rose from her chair, her cup of coffee untouched. "I'd better go." The hand she ran through her dark hair trembled. "There isn't much time." Quickening her steps to the front door, she opened it and fled down the stairs without a backward glance.

In her rooms, she paced the floor. She had to have the money to see for herself if the man in Mexico was Jarod. Her future depended on it. She couldn't bear the limbo her life was in. If only she knew one way or the other, she would either be forced to lay her dreams of a future with Jarod to rest or they would be married. If she had no possibility of a future with Jarod, then she would be free to . . . to what? Why did Roman come to mind? Would she be free to enjoy Roman's caresses, to feel a wild excitement when his long hard body pressed against hers, to feel the hammering of her silly heart when he was near? No! Of course not. Her feelings for Jarod were deep and genuine, while for Roman she felt only . . . what? Excitement? A ridiculous animal attraction? Or was there more? Hadn't she reacted deeply to his marriage proposal? Might she not have considered it happily if they had loved each other? But they didn't. Roman loved Elleen, and she loved Jarod.

Jarod! She had to get that money, and Roman seemed like the only possibility. She had exhausted every other means of acquiring it. There was no one she could ask. For a fleeting moment it occurred to her to ask Shirle. Hurrying to the front door, she put her hand on the doorknob, and then she let it go. Shirle wouldn't understand, she decided. She was too liberated to see anything wrong with Shannon modeling for Roman for the money. She couldn't ask Shirle. She didn't even want Shirle to know that Jarod might be in Mexico. The fewer people who knew, the better. Roman had made her feel like a fool when she told him that Jarod might be alive but hadn't tried to contact her. She was sure that if the man *was* Jarod, he had some perfectly valid explanation for not getting in touch with her, but other people might not understand her reasoning.

For a few minutes she battled with herself, but it was a battle that could end in only one way. She had to pose for Roman.

For the next hour and a half she was in agony. The more she reasoned with herself, the less she wanted to pose for him. Though she told herself that being unclothed before a man in this day and age was an ordinary experience for the majority of girls her age, it didn't alter her feelings about what she was going to do. To her, it was not only shameful and degrading, it was painfully humiliating to undress for a man. And the fact that heaven alone knew who would see her naked form on canvas made her feel violently ill.

She showered, washed her hair and curled it. The minutes seemed to fly by, and the more she dreaded her appointment, the faster time flew. Long before she had prepared herself to face Roman, it was nine o'clock. The thought of actually disrobing for him twisted her stomach in knots. When and how did one disrobe for a painting? And what did one wear to disrobe?

She yanked her clothes around in her closet, trying to decide what to wear. Suddenly she broke into almost hysterical laughter. What did it matter what she wore? She would only take it off. Deciding that a caftan would be the quickest and easiest thing to slip on and off, she indiscriminately pulled one out of her closet and donned it. It was time to go, but she stood before the mirror fussing with her hair. In the end, she swept the curls into a mass on top of her head, securing them with a red ribbon. After discreetly applying her makeup, she studied the results.

Heart pounding, ears ringing, she remembered that Roman had said that most viewers wouldn't concentrate on her face.

She trudged up the steps to his rooms, forcing her feet to make the climb until she was there. Her hand had barely touched the wood when he appeared. His hard features intimidated her even more. "So, you did make it," he growled.

Again she wondered why he seemed so angry, when he had asked her to pose. She couldn't understand it, but she already had enough things to worry about.

"Yes," she murmured, stepping inside as he held the door open for her. He had shaved and dressed in white slacks and a forest-green shirt. He was neat and his handsome looks made her feel breathless. Posing for him would be easier if he weren't so very good-looking. She glanced about the room, noting that his easel was set up, the canvas resting on it, his paints lined up alongside.

"Well, let's go to work," he said brusquely.

Fighting panic, Shannon stood rooted to the floor and took a deep determined breath. "Where do I . . . I mean, where shall I . . . undress?"

He cocked an eyebrow and looked at her with annoyance. "It really doesn't matter. Use the bedroom if you want."

Seeing her reluctance and hesitation, he snapped, "You know, Shannon, you're going to be nude before me for most of the day, but if you'll be more comfortable, come out in the robe on the back of the door. I'll study your facial structure when I position you, and then you can just slip the robe off." Stroking his strong jaw, he mused, "I think I'll have you lie on the couch." He reached out and pulled the ribbon. Her hair tumbled about her shoulders in a mass of dark curls. Lifting her chin, he turned her face first one way, then the other. "Nice. Very nice," he murmured. "Lucky Jarod."

Shannon could feel her breathing quicken. His nearness had such power over her that she found herself thinking: Lucky Elleen, to have this man in love with her. He was cruel and he was arrogant, but there was something so strong and so compelling about him that she couldn't help but think that there was much more to him than the hard side she saw. He ran a thumb along her cheek and immediately she shook the foolish thoughts from her mind. He was cold, cruel and obnoxious, and she was only imagining that there was something more to him than that. Instinctively she withdrew from his touch. Almost as if he couldn't bear to have her move, he reached for her again. Then he dropped his hand. "Time is passing," he stated impersonally. "And time is money. Get undressed."

Mechanically she went to the bedroom, shutting the door firmly behind her. When she caught sight of her pale, trembling figure in the mirror over his dresser, she was shocked. Why would the man even want to paint her? She looked so . . . so unhealthy compared to his other models. With quaking fingers she slipped the caftan over her head. It took longer to get out of her bra and panties, though she was certainly skilled in their removal. The bra suddenly seemed difficult to unhook, the panties too tight to slide down her hips.

When she was finally naked, she hid from the girl in the mirror. Her image seemed to taunt her. She looked quickly, but didn't see the robe Roman had mentioned. One of his shirts lay on a chair; she yanked it up and pulled it on, quickly buttoning each button. The shirt came down to her thighs, and she reluctantly opened the bedroom door and stepped out.

At the sight of her, Roman broke into cruel, derisive laughter. Instantly Shannon was angry. How dare he make every attempt possible to embarrass her? He knew how sensitive she was about the entire arrangement. Yet he stood there boldly mocking her. "What's so amusing?" she demanded, forgetting the picture she must present in the baggy shirt.

He made no attempt to soften his ridicule. "You," he taunted. "Not that I don't find you appealing in that shirt of mine. Your . . . your fragility is heightened in that getup, but people won't pay for it. They expect nudes from me. They're my specialty."

"And probably all you can do," she snapped, her eyes bright with fury. She had come here to model nude for him, and she would. She yanked at the shirt, jerking it over her head without undoing a single button, then flung it contemptuously to the floor. "Where do you want me?" she demanded.

The laughter was instantly wiped from his face, and she was alarmed by the look that replaced it. "I want you anywhere I can have you," he answered in a low, hoarse voice. "You're beautiful."

Her anger still brewing, it took a minute for his words to sink in. When they did, she spat at him, "If this is a trick, Mr. Morgan, you're out of luck. I came here to model, and model only. Either you paint me, or tell me your intentions are immoral and I'll leave. If you think I came here for any other purpose than to earn money to find my fiancé, you are greatly mistaken."

For that moment of anger, she forgot that she stood before him nude. The almost painful look in his eyes as they roamed hungrily over her naked body made her want to comfort him, and she

couldn't understand her own feelings. When her
words died out, the softness and vulnerability in his
eyes were replaced with the usual hard, bitter look.
Shannon immediately attempted to cover herself
with her hands. She could imagine how absurd she
looked, but she couldn't stop the defensive gesture.

"I want nothing from you but a picture," he
snarled, his gray eyes flinty with anger. "Lie on the
couch." With his index finger, he motioned her
toward the couch, but, acutely aware of her nakedness, she was frozen where she stood in her ridiculous posture.

"For heaven's sake," he growled, "you're wasting
the whole day. Will you get over here!"

Shannon couldn't. She just couldn't. Only her
anger had permitted her to display herself before the
man. Now she felt exposed and ashamed. Tears
rushed to her eyes and she shook her head, her long
dark hair tumbling forward as she reached for the
protection of his shirt lying before her. In an instant
she had pulled it over her head, hiding her curves
from him as she ran toward the bedroom. But
Roman had no intention of permitting her to escape.
Catching her at the door, he placed a restraining
hand on her arm and turned her around, pressing
her against the closed bedroom door as his lips
sought hers.

To her horror, Shannon felt herself move forward
to meet his embrace. She wanted him to hold her.
She wanted his lips to touch hers. She wanted the
hot heat of his body against hers. She knew it was
insane, but she wanted Roman Morgan!

Chapter Five

Shannon struggled to gain some control of the situation, fighting her own ardor as well as his. She felt an excited panic as her body made contact with his. Resisting an impulse to wrap her arms around him, she kept them pressed to her sides until she felt a teasing sensation on her naked thighs. She grabbed his hands, clinging to them to stop the torment of their fiery touch. As his lips moved from her mouth to her throat, he easily freed his hands to slide them up under the shirt, scorching her stomach as he stroked the tender skin. With a gasp, she realized that he had found her breasts and was fondling them gently. A battle raged within her. What was she doing, letting Roman hold her like this, letting him fan the flame of hot desire running through her? She tried to think of Jarod, but instead she heard herself moan softly.

To hide her own confusion and desire, she twisted to free herself from Roman's grasp. When he moved his head away from the hollow of her throat, she slapped him hard across the face. For an instant she saw disbelief mirrored in the soft gray of his eyes, and she wanted to pull him to her and kiss away the sting of her hand.

But it was too late. Hate edged his scornful voice. "If you really have a fiancé hiding in Mexico, I suggest you leave him there." He stepped back from

her and she saw the imprint of her hand on his
cheek.

In a tiny voice she murmured, "Why?"

He snorted at the question. "Come, come. You
don't need to ask. The reason is obvious." His eyes
raked suggestively over her body, resting for a
moment on the rapid rise and fall of her breasts
beneath the baggy shirt.

"You're mistaken," she protested. "I love Jarod."

"Then I pity the poor fool," Roman mocked.

"I know what you must be thinking," Shannon
cried, "but you're wrong. I . . . I didn't want you to
kiss me. You . . . you forced yourself on me. I don't
want your attentions, I assure you. You take advantage of me. You overpower me. I really do love
Jarod. Do you think I'd go to such desperate
measures . . . as . . . as posing for you if I didn't?
Do you think I'd humiliate myself this way here with
you?"

His voice was cynical. "That statement sounds
rather familiar. Isn't that a paraphrase of what
Elleen said in the restaurant? Frankly, I don't think
either of you knows what you want." His eyes were
cold as they traveled over her face.

"I can't speak for your . . . your friend," Shannon said in an anguished voice, "but I want Jarod.
I'm desperate to find him. Don't you understand
that? I've been worried sick about him for months."

A cruel smile twisted Roman's lips. "Worried sick
about him until another man takes you in his arms."

"That's not true," she denied passionately. "I'd
give anything to be with Jarod now instead of you.
You don't know what goes on inside my heart. I'd do
anything to have Jarod back," she finished in a
choked voice.

One uneven brow arched up. "Anything?"

Her chin thrust forward, she looked at him defensively. She wouldn't back down before him again. "You heard me," she retorted, the words catching in her throat.

He rocked back on his heels, and he seemed to consider her statement. She held her breath. What would he say this time?

"I'll make a deal with you, Shannon," he said. "If you love Jarod as much as you say, it won't hurt you to accept it. If you find him, you have what you want. If you don't find him, I have what I want, which shouldn't matter to you, since Jarod can never be yours anyway if he can't be found."

Her heart increased its rapid pace. "What's the deal?" she asked almost fearfully.

"I'll finance the trip to Mexico. I'll even go with you and the detective to the pickup point. If you find Jarod alive, I'll use my money and whatever influence I have to see that he gets a fair deal on his return. If this man in Mexico isn't Jarod, you marry me. Chances are excellent that Jarod isn't going to be found if this isn't your man, in which case you may as well marry me as any man. I won't ask for your love."

Shannon felt faint. "What do you mean?"

"Do I have to spell everything out for you?" he growled bitterly. "It will be just as I told you before. I won't touch you." He smiled bitterly. "I won't want to. And perhaps Elleen will see the futility of chasing me when I'm safely married. Things might settle between her and my father." He dismissed his thoughts with a wave of his hand. "Regardless, your love for your beloved missing Jarod can remain shut up in your frigid heart. If you find yourself attracted to another man, say, after a year, you'll be free to go. I'll settle a handsome amount of money on you, and that will be that."

"Just like that?" she asked resentfully.

"Just like that."

"I don't understand," she murmured quietly. "If you want a wife, why don't you find someone you will love and who can return your love?"

His look was scornful. "I've explained to you that Elleen will believe ours is a real marriage. Other than that, I see no need to waste my time with an emotion like love. My life will be my own, as will yours, as long as you're discreet. I won't hold you to any marriage vows. If you find that sacred love you profess for Jarod crumbling, you're free to do as you please."

Shannon was more hurt than outraged, and she didn't understand the pain she felt. "I'd never marry under those circumstances. Besides, what if this man isn't Jarod, but Sam locates Jarod later. What good would your deal do me then? How would I explain your . . . generosity to Jarod?"

Roman's face stiffened into an angry mask. "Quite simply, my pet. You would explain that I never touched you and that you did what you did out of love for him. I assure you, our marriage will be only on paper. I won't approach you unless you invite me to. I wouldn't dream of violating your temple to Jarod. If he's all you claim, he'll be honored indeed that you made such a sacrifice for him."

Torn by conflicting emotions she neither knew how to deal with nor how to understand, Shannon searched her mind for some reply. It did make sense, didn't it? How could she be hurt by the deal if it was as Roman said? How could she turn down such a chance to find Jarod? If the man in Mexico was Jarod, all of her longing and heartache and uncertainty would end. She could wipe Roman out of her mind. If the man wasn't Jarod and she was faced with marrying Roman, she would have to cross that bridge when she came to it.

She refused to even consider the crazy way her heart beat at the thought of marriage to him. He made it very plain that he would require nothing of her but that she appear to be his wife. It was really all quite simple, the way he explained it. Then why couldn't she reply? It all came down to one thing, didn't it? And that one thing was Jarod. This was her chance to end a year of agony. She had to know if the man in Mexico was her fiancé. She had to. There was nothing else involved. Then why did her heart pound so at the prospect of marriage to Roman? Was it only because she took marriage so very seriously? Or was there something more? For as long as she could remember, she had known exactly what she wanted from marriage. She wanted a strong and abiding love that would endure through the years, and she had seen Jarod in the role of husband in such a marriage. Never had she considered marriage to a handsome, volatile man like Roman who could send her senses reeling with a mere glance. Instead of a quiet, enduring, comfortable companionship, a girl would find herself thrown into a passionate, fiery existence with such a man. No, that wasn't for her. But then, Roman hadn't offered her a real marriage, and Shannon was only considering his offer because of Jarod.

"I accept your deal," she said, her lips quivering slightly as she looked at him. No longer able to meet his gaze, she lowered her eyes.

Roman placed a hand under her chin, forcing her to meet his eyes. "You agree to all of the deal? If this man isn't Jarod, we'll be married as soon as we return from the trip."

She nodded, fighting down the panic that rose in

her throat. When she saw the angry, bitter look surface in his eyes, she was puzzled. If this was what he wanted, why did her agreement make him so angry?

Releasing her, he suggested curtly that she get dressed. She hurried into the bedroom and pulled her clothes on. She was caught between mounting excitement and a terrible feeling of dread.

Nervously she stepped out of the bedroom and walked to the living room, where Roman was busy at his easel. When she approached, he quickly covered the canvas so that she was unable to see what he was working on. She wasn't interested anyway. She had too many other things on her mind to worry about what Roman was painting.

"Why don't you arrange a meeting with Sam Harvard in your apartment for the three of us?" he suggested. "I want to know what information he's going on, and we can tell him that I've taken an interest in the case. You can inform him that I'm going to finance the Mexico expedition. There will be no need, of course, to tell him about the arrangement between you and me."

Shannon shrugged her shoulders, trying to affect nonchalance. When she tried to speak, it took her several seconds to get the words out. "Whatever you think," she agreed. "I'll make the meeting for tonight if Sam's available. He did stress the need for haste."

"Fine."

Roman propped himself against a chair back and looked at Shannon. She didn't know what else to say, and she gripped her hands behind her back as she stood before him. If the man was Jarod, the situation would be resolved. If the man wasn't Jarod, then she would have to confront Roman on a more personal basis. Much more personal. For now, she wanted no more to do with him. "I'll go and make the arrangements, then," she murmured, stepping toward the door. She was relieved that he said nothing more and made no move to stop her.

She walked down the steps on shaky legs. It all seemed so crazy. She prayed that her decision to let Roman finance the trip was the right one. She hoped even more that his word was good. After all, she knew so little about the man. If Jarod couldn't be found and she became Roman's bride, how drastically would her life change? She didn't want to think about it. She couldn't think about it. It was frightening. She went into her apartment and phoned Sam's office while she still had the nerve.

When she had explained what she wanted, he told her he would see her at about seven. How on earth would she occupy herself for the rest of the day? She thought she would go insane if she had to stay inside all day. She slipped a note under Roman's door to tell him about the meeting, too shaken to face him. Back downstairs, a growling in her stomach reminded her that she had eaten very little. She took a jar of peanut butter and a jar of blackberry preserves and made her favorite sandwich. Then, taking a sweater from her closet, she hurried out onto the beach with her meal in hand.

Walking along the sandy shore, nibbling on the sandwich, she tried to ready herself mentally for the task ahead of her. Her destiny suddenly seemed out of her control. Any way she looked at it, it was in Roman Morgan's hands. For a couple of hours she paced the beach, her thoughts in turmoil. So many problems faced her if she didn't find Jarod, and maybe if she did find him. Sam had tried to prepare her for the possibility that Jarod's appearance would bring more trouble, but she couldn't make herself believe that. She found herself wandering out on the old Newport Beach Pier, staring down into the ocean waters. *Was* it possible that Jarod had staged his drowning?

Small doubts ate at her. Was it conceivable that she didn't know Jarod as well as she thought? What would she do if he *had* been involved in the crime? Would that in any way change her love for him? She simply didn't see how that was possible. She and Jarod had planned a lifetime together. She really couldn't believe that any of the acts he was accused of had been premeditated. Sam couldn't possibly be right. Jarod wasn't hiding from her, and it was unthinkable that he would run from her.

And what about Roman's assertion that Jarod could have found some way to contact her, regardless of his circumstances, if he really loved her? Shannon knew that Jarod would solve the puzzle when she saw him. She wouldn't allow Sam or Roman to shake her faith in him or in his love. They didn't know Jarod as she did. She was sure everything would work itself out if only she could be in Jarod's arms again. She would forget all about Roman and the crazy way she felt when he was near.

The dinner hour was fast approaching when she finally left the pier and strolled back to the house. As she neared, she looked up to see Roman watching her from his balcony. Wondering just how long he had been there, she deliberately lowered her eyes and entered the main door without speaking to him. She would be glad when the entire venture was behind her.

After she made herself a hot meal, she put on a pot of coffee and sat down to await the arrival of the two men. Roman came before seven, and Shannon let him in apprehensively. She had wanted Sam to come first. As soon as she had given Roman a cup of coffee, she was relieved to hear another knock. She opened the door for Sam and quickly ushered him in.

She was vaguely self-conscious when she made the introductions. The two men had met the day Roman had used her phone, but she had neglected to introduce them. Each eyed the other with suspicion.

"Just what is this all about?" Sam asked. "I wasn't aware that you were an interested party, Mr. Morgan."

"'Roman,' if you will," he insisted, sitting back down on the couch and taking a sip of his coffee. His eyes met Shannon's, and she felt embarrassed. "Everything Miss Andrews does interests me, Mr. Harvard."

"I see," Sam commented. But it was obvious that he didn't see at all. He found something a bit peculiar about the alliance between Shannon and Roman, but he had been a detective too long to expose his hand before he got a feel for the game. "Call me Sam, Roman." Settling himself into a nearby chair, he asked, "What can I do for you?"

"I want to know all about the meeting in Mexico. As an interested party, I'll finance the trip and any expenses that you incur. Feel free to come to me for any sum," Roman stated bluntly.

Sam's eyes moved to Shannon and flicked over her momentarily as though he were trying to access the new development. "I see," he commented dryly as his eyes met Roman's again.

Shannon had the depressing feeling that he really did see now. Was it so obvious that she must be giving Roman something in return for his money? Whether it was or not, her shame caused a blush to rise on her cheeks. Sam briefed Roman about the contact in Mexico. Then he looked at Shannon.

Her face a mask of detachment, she met his gaze. "When can we leave? How soon can the contact be reached?"

"We can leave early in the morning. Three o'clock should do it. We'll catch Jarod, if the man *is* Jarod, before he gets out of bed. That is, if it's agreeable to you both."

Shannon and Roman's eyes met, and they nodded.

"All set, then," Sam said, standing up. "I guess that's it. I assume you know the other details concerning our quarry, Roman, or do you want me to fill you in?"

Roman shook his head. "Shannon's done that." Reaching into his back pocket, he pulled out his wallet. To Shannon's surprise, he brought out a number of crisp hundred-dollar bills. "I understand you need two thousand dollars to start. Is that correct?"

Sam's face carefully concealed any emotion. "That should cover it." Giving Shannon a brief look, he took the money and walked toward the front door. "Well, I have things to do. Be ready on time in the morning. I don't want this bird to fly. He's been too difficult to cage. Bring gear for a couple of days in case something goes wrong and we have to wait or follow him."

"Thank you, Sam," Shannon said, opening the door for him. She stayed by it after he left, waiting for Roman to follow him. When she saw that he wasn't going to budge from the couch, she closed the door reluctantly and returned to her chair. "Shouldn't we get to bed since we have to get such an early start tomorrow?" she asked, trying to avoid the piercing look in his eyes.

"Not getting cold feet about our agreement, are you?" he asked harshly.

"Are you?" she snapped. She knew he was angry

again, but she didn't know why. It was *his* deal. It
had been the same with the posing. He asked her to
do it, and then he seemed angry because she agreed.
"What is it with you?" she demanded. "You want
me to do these outlandish things, and then you snap
and snarl when I say I will. If you don't want me to
do them, why do you ask?"

His stormy gray eyes stared at her. "I really don't
know. Maybe it just surprises me that you'll go to
such lengths for your precious boyfriend. I wonder,
Shannon, if he'll be impressed with the sacrifices
you're making for him in the name of love. Will he
ever know that you've undressed for his cause, or
that you may marry for it?"

Shannon controlled the anger she felt toward
Roman. Why did he insist on making the situation so
tense? She didn't know how she would see it to the
end. In a tight little voice she said, "Why don't you
leave so that I can get some sleep, Roman? I think
that would be best."

Suddenly he marched over to her chair and
gripped her shoulders. "Do you think so, Shannon?
Funny, I thought you might be concerned about
your future. Our future together. Don't you want to
know what you can expect from your life with me? I
should think you'd at least be curious. You just may
find yourself married to me in a few days."

Yes! she wanted to cry. Yes, I want to know about
my future with you. Yes, I want to know about our
marriage. But she dared not let herself think about
it, let alone talk about it with Roman. Her primary
concern was Jarod, she forced herself to remember.
Besides, she knew Roman was angry with her and
only taunting her for some sin she didn't even know
she had committed. He must have loved Elleen very
deeply, she thought, to carry such hatred inside
him. She shook her head slowly. "No, Roman. I

don't want to know. I'm confident that the man in Mexico will be Jarod. Tomorrow will be the day I begin to forget all about you."

Roman's laugh was short and bitter. "You won't forget about me, Shannon. I'll see to that. I intend to marry you immediately after the return trip."

Before Shannon could reply, he released her and left the room. She sat there on her chair for a long time, staring at the door, her arms burning where his fingers had bitten into them. What *would* her future be with Roman Morgan?

The ringing of the alarm clock awakened her after what seemed like only minutes, not hours. Struggling into full consciousness, she began to picture the trip she was about to make. The reality of what she would face suddenly became depressing. What if the man wasn't Jarod, and she was forced to marry Roman Morgan?

Angrily she slid out of bed, stalked to her closet and took out the clothes she had planned to wear. In the chilly darkness of the early morning, she dressed quickly. She made herself a cup of coffee, feeling the need for the hot stimulant. She had a sense of approaching doom as she prepared for the trip across the border. She couldn't explain why, but she felt uneasy about it. Where was her eager anticipation at the prospect of finding Jarod? It seemed to have vanished in the early-morning reality of the uncertainty ahead.

Sam arrived promptly at three A.M. Shannon, though sleepy and edgy, was ready and waiting. She heard Roman's steps on the stairs at the same time as she opened the door for Sam. The men decided that they would travel in Roman's car, and Sam helped Roman load the bags in the trunk.

When they were ready to leave, Shannon started to climb into the backseat, but Roman grabbed her arm, indicating that Sam should sit in the back. Giving Roman an angry look, Shannon waited until Sam got in, then permitted Roman to guide her into the front beside him.

Sam gave Roman directions to the rendezvous point and they started out. When they had been under way for a few minutes, Shannon was surprised to receive no answer when she spoke to the detective. She looked over her shoulder to find that he had drifted off into a sound sleep. Hugging the door on the passenger side, she could think of nothing to say to Roman, and she was grateful that he didn't attempt to make conversation.

Sam stirred briefly when, sometime later, they crossed the border into colorful Tijuana, Mexico, but he soon went back to sleep without comment. Shannon glanced absently at the shops, closed and quiet in the early-morning coolness. She recalled other times when she had been in the town and it had been filled with activity as tourists and natives mingled. She lapsed into thought as Roman drove farther into Mexico.

Later, when they approached a quiet village, Roman woke Sam. Shannon was startled by the detective's immediate awareness of his surroundings. Giving Roman directions to a small adobe café where they were to meet their contact, he started searching the surrounding area. Shannon was sure his perceptive eyes didn't miss a detail. He seemed satisfied that everything was as it should be when they climbed out of the car to enter the café, which was already open for business.

After they had sat down on rickety red chairs, Sam ordered coffee for each of them. As it was served, he

asked the proprietor a few questions in halting
Spanish. The man answered and left, and Sam
turned to Roman and Shannon.

"It appears that everything is on schedule. The
café owner knows Rafael Reyes, our contact. He
says Rafael is in town, but that no *gringo* resides in
this village. That's as it should be. I told you our
quarry is in hiding. Rafael is supposed to meet us at
seven o'clock. The house where our boy is staying is
on the outskirts of this village."

Shannon felt a tightening in the pit of her stomach. This sort of intrigue wasn't up her alley, and she
thought of Shirle. A writer would appreciate an
adventure like this. She felt only a terrible anxiety to
see if this man was Jarod. She felt that she was close
to the end of her year's search, and yet she was
aware that the trip could be a wild-goose chase.
"Sam, do you think Jarod will be there?" she asked,
her lips trembling.

Sam shrugged. "That's what we're counting on."

Shannon looked at her watch. It was a few minutes
until seven. She took another sip of her coffee and it
burned all the way down to her stomach. Taking a
deep breath, Shannon slowly let it escape her lips.
Would the minutes ever pass? She wished it was all
over. Now that they had actually reached their
destination, she found her excitement at a new high.
Goose bumps played on her skin and she could
almost feel Jarod's presence, she was so excited
about seeing him. Roman hadn't said a word, and
Shannon didn't look in his direction. She didn't want
to know what he was thinking. Sam kept peering out
the café window and watching time tick by on his
wristwatch. When seven o'clock arrived, so did a
swarthy Mexican of undetermined age.

"*Hola!*" he said as he approached their table.
"*Señor* Sam Harvard?"

"Sí. Qué tal?" Sam responded. When the man replied, Sam indicated a chair. "This is our man, Rafael," he said to Shannon and Roman.

"Buenos días," Rafael greeted them. Roman nodded and Shannon tried to smile at him. She knew a few random words of Spanish because it was spoken by a large percentage of California's population, but she didn't feel like trying her knowledge out on this man.

Rafael nodded and joined them at the table, but he confined his conversation to Sam. Time continued to tick by, and Shannon squirmed in her chair. What were they waiting for? If they wanted to catch Jarod in bed, why didn't they leave? Sam seemed to share her thoughts. He suddenly jumped up from the table and cursed. Yanking Rafael up by the shirt collar, he dragged him off his chair. A brief scuffle ensued and some harsh words were exchanged. The owner of the café rushed over and spoke sharply to them in rapid Spanish, obviously ordering them out of his building.

In a flurry of footsteps, they hurried outside, with Sam still gripping Rafael's collar. Even though Shannon didn't understand the words that were spoken, she knew that something had gone wrong.

"Blast!" Sam muttered savagely. "We've been double-crossed. Rafael told our boy that we were coming. He wanted to work both sides of the street. Our boy paid him to keep us away until he could escape, which I assume he is in the process of doing at this very moment. Now Rafael wants to double-cross him, for more money, of course. If we increase our sum to a thousand, plus the reward money, he'll take us to the man now."

Sam shook Rafael roughly. In return, the man glared at him and spat a stream of harsh-sounding Spanish words.

"Don't bicker with him," Roman said. "Time is of the essence." He pulled out his wallet and handed Rafael a thick stack of bills. Then, to everyone's surprise, he spoke quickly in fluent Spanish to Rafael. With Rafael leading and giving directions, they all rushed to Roman's car. Rafael pointed to the left, speaking hurriedly. When they had gone a short distance, he gestured to a dumpy little house partially sheltered from the road by huge trees. Even as they drove toward the house, a tall blond man with a beard was climbing hastily into an old car with a beautiful Mexican woman. Roman swerved his car to the right, blocking their exit.

While Shannon strained to get a good look at the man, she saw the woman grab his arm and cling tightly to it as he started the car. Turning to reassure her, he gave her a quick kiss on the lips. Shannon was able to see him well then. But she couldn't believe her eyes. "Jarod! It *is* Jarod!" she cried. She jerked the door open and ran toward the vehicle.

"Jarod!" she cried. "Jarod!"

As she reached his side, Jarod rolled up the window, put the car in reverse and backed up several feet. Suddenly the car made a quick turn and drove off in the opposite direction at high speed. For a few seconds Shannon stared after it in disbelief. Jarod had driven off! He had seen her and driven off! He had actually run from her! He *had* been hiding out here in Mexico, mere hours from her, *with a woman!* She had been at home waving his innocence like a banner, mourning his loss, and he had been hiding, safe and well! A huge wave of disappointment swept over her, quickly followed by a slow anger which burned in the pit of her stomach and spread like wildfire through her.

She was amazed to realize that more than any-thing she felt anger because Jarod had lied to her and run from her, rather than hurt because he was with another woman. Everyone had been right about Jarod. Sam had been right about Jarod. Even Roman Morgan had been right about Jarod, and that hurt most of all. She had staunchly defended him, and why?

Well, she was glad he had driven off, she told herself bitterly. Now that she saw the man Jarod really was, she was ashamed that she had ever imagined that she loved him. She had always felt that he had been misunderstood by everyone. Misunderstood indeed! She was the one who had been fooled—by him! And to have him embarrass her so horribly here like this . . . She stood there in the dirt road, powerless to move, even though the car had disappeared in a cloud of dust. Bitter tears of hurt and humiliation welled up in her eyes and trickled down her cheeks.

She gasped as Roman stepped up to her. A sob caught in her throat as she stared up at his angry face. Gripping her arm fiercely, he virtually dragged her back up the road. "Stop behaving like a senseless fool!" he demanded. "He's not worth it!"

Shannon twisted to free herself, but his grip was too strong. "Let go of me!" she spat at him.

"I told you to leave him here in Mexico!" he growled. "Now, control yourself before I slap you. Where is your pride? He doesn't want you!"

And I don't want him! she almost cried, but she would die before she would admit to Roman that he had been right all along. "You wouldn't dare slap me!" she gasped, struggling to be free of him.

"I swear I will if you don't compose yourself immediately," he snarled, his face rigid with anger.

Shannon saw Sam approaching and tried to run to him, but Roman kept her at his side. Fastening his arm about her shoulders like a vise, he marched her toward the car. Sam walked along with them, waiting until Roman had literally shoved her into the car before he spoke. Shannon wasn't surprised to see that Rafael had disappeared.

"So, it *was* Jarod," Sam said.

Shannon couldn't look at him. She didn't want anyone to pity her for her involvement with Jarod. She had been duped by him, and that realization was painful enough. "Yes," she admitted tightly.

"Well, that dirty . . . I'm sorry, Shannon," he replied gruffly. "I tried to prepare you. This sort of thing happens every day. It happens to wives as well as sweethearts. I wish there was more I could say to you. I don't imagine you'll want me to track him down again after this."

She shook her head, just wanting to forget about the whole event. She was relieved that it was finally over. There would be no more waiting and wondering about Jarod. She was sure that it was better that it had worked out this way: Jarod was alive—for that she was grateful; but she was through with him—and for that she was also grateful. But right now she was too ashamed and embarrassed to want to talk about it.

Shannon huddled in the corner of her seat for the ride back to Newport Beach, hoping that no one would mention Jarod again. She felt the bitter tears fill her eyes again, and she covered her face with her hands, trying to hold back their inevitable escape. For a whole year she had prayed, longed, dreamed and waited for Jarod. And for a whole year, or longer, he had really been dead to her. He had never loved her as he had vowed, or he couldn't have run to another woman's arms so quickly. She was suddenly shocked to realize that she had no right to judge Jarod in that respect. She had found a pleasure in Roman's arms which she had never known in

Jarod's. Glancing at him, a terrible revelation dawned on her: the very worst aspect of this fiasco was that Roman Morgan had been there to see it all. If she lived a thousand years, it wouldn't be long enough to live down the shame she had felt there on that narrow little dirt road today.

Roman slanted his moody gray eyes at her, and she hid her face behind her arm, praying that the trip would soon end. Neither of the men spoke to her again as the car wound its way back home. When they finally arrived at Blue Haven, Sam went to his own car and Roman walked into the house. Shannon's legs felt leaden and heavy and her head was throbbing. A flush colored her face when she thought about her conversation with Roman, and the lengths she had gone to for the money to search for Jarod. She had been such a fool!

Roman followed her into her apartment, and Shannon, squaring her shoulders, turned to face him. "Don't worry. I'll live up to my side of the deal. I'll marry you tomorrow or whenever, but right now . . . right now, will you please just leave me alone?" Her shoulders drooped again as she turned to walk toward her bedroom. She wished the floor would swallow her.

Catching her by the arm, Roman dragged her back to him. "Our deal was that we would marry if no trace of Jarod was found. You were so sure if we found him that he would return with you that I didn't include the possibility of him actually running away. Since I didn't include that possibility, and we did find him, I won't force you into marriage."

For a moment Shannon could only stand and stare at him. She was already reconciled to the marriage. What did it matter now anyway? She had no way to repay the money he had used to finance the search. And she had expected to marry him if Jarod wasn't found. And for her Jarod hadn't been found. She didn't even know the stranger who had run away like a scared rabbit. She might as well marry Roman; she would never trust a man again anyway.

Her eyes met his, and she was alarmed by the frantic beating of her heart. "Jarod didn't return with me. A deal is a deal. If you want the marriage, I'll marry you. It doesn't really make any difference now."

She was too confused by her own agitation at the prospect of Roman calling off the marriage to try to understand the anger that hardened his features. "Fine. We'll discuss it tomorrow."

Shannon watched as he closed the door. Tonight she would weep alone in her bed for a love that had never been hers. Tomorrow she would make plans to marry a stranger whose love never *could* be hers.

Chapter Six

When Shannon awakened the next morning, her eyes were swollen and puffy after crying herself to sleep. Jarod's role in her life was over. After the shock and the shame had subsided, she felt only a dull anger at his deceitful behavior. Jarod *was* irresponsible—and a criminal to boot! She was well rid of him; she hadn't known him at all. He had cleverly fooled her with his sweet words and his "little-boy" behavior, and then he had left her behind while he sought solace in another woman's arms. After she had all but sold her soul to search for him, he had run from her! He had stepped on the gas pedal and vanished without a single word!

Well, he was out of her life now. She shook her head, amazed at the tremendous relief she felt at this knowledge. It was as if a terrible burden had been lifted from her shoulders. A fact she had refused to face blossomed in her mind. She had been afraid that she didn't love Jarod from the minute he had been accused of the crime, and for a brief moment she, too, had doubted his innocence. Then she had felt so guilty and so disloyal that she had instantly stifled her doubt and defended him more strongly than any evidence had warranted.

The thought brought a scarlet tint to her cheeks. All that was behind her now. She was Roman Morgan's and she would have to make the best of it.

The wedding she had dreamed of would be to a man who had a score to settle. She would only be an instrument of revenge, not love. But it didn't matter, did it?

She recalled his harsh words. He had mocked the way she had wept over Jarod, thinking that she was heartbroken, not humiliated to the depth of her being. Well, let him think that she still loved Jarod. He still loved Elleen. He found Shannon's actions disgusting, but not disgusting enough to keep him from using marriage to her for his purposes. The thought caused a strange ache in her heart, but there were no more tears. She was all cried out. Swinging her legs over the side of the bed, she stood up a little unsteadily and made her way to the kitchen. She knew she had to force herself to eat something. Roman was going to talk to her today about the marriage.

After she had eaten, she felt a little better. A shower helped, too, though nothing could ease her emotional torment.

She went back to her apartment, dressed in the first thing that came to hand and sat down on the couch to wait. If she knew Roman at all, she wouldn't have to wait long. He would be here soon enough to stake his claim. Roman had only appeared in her life a few days ago, and yet it seemed as if weeks had passed. Her life had been a whirlwind of emotion, anger, pain and conflicting events since his arrival.

In less than ten minutes she heard his knock on her door. "Come in," she called out dryly, sure it would be Roman.

He stepped into the room and surveyed her dispassionately. She glanced at him, seeing that he was dressed all in brown, the color deepening his dark looks. She remained seated, waiting for him to speak.

"Why don't I just make myself comfortable?" he muttered sarcastically.

In response, she gestured toward a chair.

The swift strides he took across the room revealed his anger. He dragged the chair closer to her and sat down heavily. "You look like hell," he snapped critically. "And you're behaving like a teenager." Grasping her chin tightly, he moved her face from side to side. "Tears for Jarod?" he growled. "I heard you weeping last night. And for what? A man who lied to you and left you for another woman. You're a fool!"

A smoldering anger stirred her from her apathy. Her flashing eyes met his; she was not in the mood for any abuse from him. "Don't you speak to me like that!" she demanded. "I'm not Elleen!"

He stood up abruptly. "I'm going to make arrangements for our marriage today. When you can discard your mourning long enough to function, come upstairs." With that nasty command, he turned on his heel and strode to the door, slamming it behind him as he vanished.

His antagonistic manner provoked Shannon to action. Who did he think he was? He acted as if she had no right at all to be upset with the way things had turned out! No wonder Elleen had married his father instead of him. He was an automaton with no feelings. He had no heart. He didn't care how ashamed and embarrassed she was at having found her fiancé in the arms of another woman after all she had done to find him. Springing to her feet, she stormed after him.

"Just a minute, Mr. Morgan!" she yelled, jerking the door open. "I'm ready to go now. Heaven forbid that I should take time to recover from one disaster before I fall into another. Let's get this over with!"

Turning on the steps, he slowly made his way back downstairs. "Don't sound so enthusiastic," he snarled. "You're not making such a sacrifice of yourself to me. As I see it, you're not exactly on the list of the ten most desirables."

"What do you mean by that?" she demanded.

"Need I spell it out for you?"

"If that's the way you feel about it," she retorted, "why do you want to go through with it? It *was* your idea!" Spinning around, she started to retreat into her apartment. She was just as happy to forget the whole thing. It had been a ridiculous idea anyway. She didn't know what had ever made her think the man was attractive. He had no redeeming qualities.

Hastening his steps, he grabbed her by the arm. "Oh, stop sulking. We made a deal. You know why I'm marrying you. Besides," he added more gently, "you may find that you like being married to me." Seeing her frown, he added, "I'll make no demands on you, and your life will be very easy. I want to go to Monterey at the end of the week. My home is there."

Her green eyes widened in surprise. "You mean we won't be living at Blue Haven?"

"Hardly. I can't stand the crowds. My estate is outside the city limits on twenty acres bordering the ocean. It's beautiful and somewhat isolated. I'm sure you'll like it."

Shannon was puzzled. She knew so little about him. She hadn't anticipated leaving Blue Haven. She wasn't quite sure what she had expected, but this wasn't it. Lowering her eyes, she studied her hands.

"Don't look as if I'm punishing you," he said in a tight voice, misunderstanding her anxiety. "Jarod won't come back to Blue Haven. If he did, I'm quite sure the authorities would cart him away. You're going to be my wife now, even if it's in name only. I won't have you mooning over him in my presence."

"I wasn't mooning over him!" she countered, immediately indignant. That was certainly true. She hadn't given Jarod a single thought since Roman came in. "I just didn't think we'd leave Blue Haven," she added. "It's my home. I love it. What will happen to it?"

"Nothing, if you want to keep it," he said, studying her face. "I've told you that our marriage can be as temporary as you want it to be. Why don't you rent out Blue Haven just as you have been? I'm sure the woman upstairs would be happy to keep an eye on the place for you."

Not knowing what else to do, Shannon nodded. It sounded reasonable enough, and she would have that additional money coming in for her future.

"Are you ready to go now?" he asked.

Shannon nodded again. She was as ready as she would ever be.

The wedding ceremony was planned for Friday night, with the trip to Monterey scheduled for the following Saturday morning. After the arrangements were made, Roman did some shopping, and he and Shannon had lunch. When they returned home, Roman suggested that they inform Shirle and Mrs. Angel of their plans.

Shannon knocked on Shirle's door and asked her to accompany them up to Mrs. Angel's apartment, explaining that she had a surprise for both of them. She didn't realize what their reaction would be until they all were sitting in Mrs. Angel's living room with the two women staring at her expectantly.

"I know it's sudden," she murmured, feeling it best to be blunt and get it over with, "but Roman and I are getting married." As soon as she saw the shock on both their faces, she realized that they had expected news of Jarod.

"You and Roman?" Shirle breathed. "How? When? Why?"

The smile Shannon tried to hold on her lips faltered. She shrugged her shoulders, but it was Roman who spoke. "Who can explain love?" he asked with a laugh.

Mrs. Angel came to Shannon's rescue, hurrying to plant a kiss on the girl's cheek. "Who indeed? My dear, we couldn't be happier for you."

"Of course," Shirle chimed in, sounding not at all certain. "It's just such a surprise."

Shannon was afraid that one of the women would mention Jarod, and in an attempt to change the subject, she said hurriedly, "What I'm really wondering is whether you would be willing to keep an eye on the building for me, Mrs. Angel. It would entail renting out the apartments and forwarding the money to me in Monterey. That's where Roman's home is," she explained. "The rest of the handling of the building can be managed from there."

Mrs. Angel patted her hand. "I'd be happy to, my dear. Pansy and I really don't have enough to do."

"I'd be very grateful," Shannon said. "I thought perhaps you could take a rent reduction for managing the building. Would that be satisfactory?"

"Why, that would be fine. Just fine," the old woman agreed, smiling.

"Good." Shannon stood up, looking at Roman to see if he was ready to leave. "Well, if you'll excuse us, we have a lot to do before the wedding and the move up the coast."

"Hey, just a minute!" Shirle insisted, hopping up from the couch as Roman started toward the door. "When is the ceremony, and may we come?"

Shannon twisted her hair with trembling fingers. "It will be Friday night." She looked hesitantly at Roman, but he said nothing. "I . . . we . . . yes, of course you can come if you want to." It was the very last thing she wanted. She had hoped for a simple little exchange of vows that would be nothing more than a formality. But she didn't know how to refuse Shirle's request.

"So soon?" Shirle exclaimed before a frown from Mrs. Angel silenced her. "Well, I insist that you allow me to take you out to dinner afterward. This calls for a celebration." She smiled broadly at Shannon.

When Shannon looked at Roman, she saw him give Shirle one of his rare, charming smiles. "We'll be very pleased to accept, won't we, darling?"

The endearment caught Shannon by surprise, and having no choice but to agree, she nodded.

The wedding took place in a small local church at seven o'clock Friday night with only Shirle and Mrs. Angel in attendance. Both women were beautifully dressed for the occasion, and Shannon felt a little ashamed of the plain beige dress she had donned for her marriage. In contrast to her haphazard attire, Roman's was flawless. Her eyes flicked over him as he stood beside her dressed in a deep green suit. She hadn't felt the need to buy a new gown. After all, it wasn't a real wedding. But she seemed to be the only one who was aware of that fact.

As Shirle had desired, they went to a nice restaurant for dinner after the ceremony. Holding up her wineglass, Shirle said warmly, "May this night be just the beginning of thousands of wonderful nights for you. Congratulations!"

Shannon's eyes met her husband's as she held her glass to her lips, and she was surprised by his happy

smile. He was so deceitful, she thought, and
so . . . so charming.

"Well, what will you do when you get back to
Monterey?" Shirle asked Roman.

"Paint," he said with a smile. "I do my best work
in my own studio."

"I'm sure you do," she agreed. "There's no place
like home, I always say. I can research anywhere,
but I want my own little rooms to write in. What
name do you paint under, Roman?"

"Lopez. It was my mother's maiden name."

Shirle raised incredulous eyes to Shannon, but
Shannon didn't understand what prompted the other
woman's excitement. "Not *the* Lopez?" she questioned.

Roman's smile was faintly indulgent. "I don't
know about *the* Lopez," he commented wryly, "but
I do use that signature on my paintings. My nudes
receive the most attention. Does your recognition of
the name mean you're familiar with any of them?"

"Indeed it does," Shirle breathed. "And I'm very
pleased to meet you. I mean," she said with a laugh,
"to know that I know you."

Shannon looked blankly at Shirle. She didn't
know much about paintings, and she wasn't familiar
with the name Lopez.

Shirle was astonished. "You can't mean that
you've married him and you don't know about his
work?" she asked. "His paintings receive interna-
tional acclaim. I have a writer friend who purchased
a nude against a background of brilliant oranges and
reds only after weeks of negotiating. The painting
was well worth it. It's breathtaking!"

"*Lady on Fire*," Roman said modestly. "One of
my favorites."

Shannon looked from one to the other in embarrassment. She had assumed that Roman was a

third-rate painter at best. She had called him a voyeur. If Shirle hadn't know his painting name, she probably would still be thinking that he was an unknown.

"And to think," Shirle breathed, "you didn't want to pose for him, Shannon."

The memory of that day she had stood naked before Roman made her blush. She was very conscious of him sitting beside her. And she was afraid of what he might say.

He smiled and winked. "It's just as well. Now that she's my wife, I don't want anyone to see her without clothes on but me."

The other two women looked at each other and laughed lightly, but Shannon turned away in embarrassment. Surely Roman didn't intend to see her unclothed either. That was what he had agreed to, a wife in name only.

She shivered at the thought of being held in his arms like a real wife, remembering the way her skin had danced to his touch. After trusting Jarod, she had been hurt by him. She could imagine how Roman would treat her if she opened up to his seductive advances. Besides, she reminded herself sharply, he had stressed the fact that he wouldn't approach her again.

She lifted her eyes, and her mouth curved at some witty remark Shirle was making to Roman, but the smile was superficial. Her heart was frozen inside her. She had already been one man's fool this week, and here she was contemplating repeating the mistake. She would see to it that Roman kept his word. Their marriage would never get into the bedroom.

"Where are you honeymooning?" Mrs. Angel asked, her cheerful voice breaking into Shannon's thoughts.

She looked at the woman and saw that she was

expected to answer the question. She turned to Roman for a response. His face remained impassive as he watched her. Her eyes pleaded with him to let her off the hook. Of course, she had no idea where they would honeymoon. "I . . ." She faltered. "It's a surprise Roman's planned for me," she managed to say. Flashing him a false smile, she prompted, "You can tell them, darling." The last word almost stuck in her throat. "Tonight's the night anyway."

His lips moved into an ironic smile as he hesitated for a moment, adding to her discomfort. "Yes. Tonight is the night," he murmured in a husky voice. Shannon felt like kicking him, but she was unable to do anything but blush.

"I can see that you have no intention of telling us," Shirle said after a brief pause. "Well, never mind. We were only curious anyway. We don't want to spoil the surprise for Shannon."

Trying to hide her feelings of discomfort, Shannon shifted in her chair. She, too, wondered where they would spend the night. Roman said they weren't leaving until tomorrow morning. Surely he didn't mean to sleep in his own apartment tonight while she slept in hers. Their separate sleeping quarters would be quite acceptable and quite desirable once they reached Monterey, but Shannon cringed at the thought of Shirle and Mrs. Angel knowing about their "deal."

Suddenly Roman announced that they would be spending the night at a hotel farther down the beach. "I don't want my bride to be weary for the journey tomorrow," he said with a twinkle in his eyes. "We're leaving in the morning."

Shannon gave him a brief smile and turned her attention to Mrs. Angel's account of her own wedding forty years ago.

Another hour passed before the two women announced that they must leave. Shannon could see from Shirle's eyes that she was already planning a new murder mystery in her head, with Roman as the main character. Both she and Mrs. Angel seemed so impressed with Roman's paintings that they could speak of little else. Shannon had seen nothing of his painting except the partially finished picture of Lena Lanet, and she certainly didn't want to comment on that. She didn't know what to expect when she and Roman went to their "honeymoon" hotel down the beach. She didn't even have a toothbrush with her, let alone nightclothes, but she was glad the evening was ending. After she had given Shirle and Mrs. Angel a nervous good-bye, she sat staring into her coffeecup.

When Roman touched her hand, she looked up in surprise. "Shall we leave, too?" he asked.

"I suppose so," Shannon sighed uncertainly.

The charm he had shown the other two women evaporated completely, and she was at a loss to understand his hostility. He walked toward the door, not even turning around to see if Shannon followed. Feeling lost, she picked up her purse and trailed along behind him.

Roman stepped into the car and waited for her to do likewise. Then, just as he had told Shirle, he drove to a hotel some distance down the beach. Without a word to her, he parked his car and got out. Coming around to her side, he opened the door. He held out his hand to her, offering her the brittlest of smiles. She let him lead her to the desk and watched as he registered them as Mr. and Mrs. Roman Morgan.

Shannon felt numb as she and Roman were led to their room by a bellhop. The room was quite lavish, but she was unable to appreciate its beauty. Her mind was racing. Was this another one of Roman's bits of trickery? Would he attempt to make love to her? There was only one bed in the room. She should have known that she couldn't trust him, she thought bitterly. Hadn't he gotten her to his room to pose for him and then forced his attentions on her? Now that Jarod was out of the picture, maybe he thought she would be eager to fall into his arms. Well, she would play second fiddle to no woman, and Elleen was the woman he really loved. Her brows drew together in a frown as she watched him settle in an easy chair.

"I'm bushed," he commented, looking at the queen-size bed critically. "I'm all for a quick shower and sleep. Tomorrow will be a busy day. What do you say? Ready for bed?"

For a moment she stared at him in disbelief. He *had* tricked her! Well, he wouldn't succeed in his plans! "Yes, I am ready for bed," she snapped, "but not with you! You can just march yourself right back down to the lobby and get another room. You're drastically mistaken if you think you're sharing that bed with me. You're not!"

If it were possible, Shannon thought his face was harsher than she had ever seen it, and she had seen some savage expressions on it. "Don't flatter yourself, Mrs. Morgan," he snapped severely. "We have a deal, one that I fully intend to honor. Climb down out of your daydreams, take a bath and get in bed. I won't touch you. However, I told you before, this marriage is going to take on *all* the appearances of a normal one, and that includes sharing a room tonight. I have no intention of making love to you, not even if that's your heart's desire!"

"Well, I assure you that it's not!" she fumed, outraged. He acted as if he thought she wanted him to make love to her and was only protesting out of pride. "I won't get in bed with you!" she flared.

His chest rose and fell with an aggravated sigh. "I won't bother you."

"You bet you won't! You won't get the chance!"

"That's fine," he declared coldly. "Sleep in a chair." Rising from his own chair, he stalked to the bathroom and slammed the door. In a couple of minutes Shannon heard the shower running. A little later she watched as he returned to the room clad in a towel. Without looking in her direction, he slipped under the bed covers, dropped the towel on the floor, flipped out the light and rolled over!

Sitting there in the dark, furious, Shannon felt like striking him. He was utterly insufferable! To her dismay, he added insult to injury by falling asleep right away; his even breathing filled the room within minutes. Leaving her sitting there in that chair hadn't bothered him at all! She had been made to suffer the degradation of Jarod's actions but she swore that Roman wouldn't get the better of her.

Stomping across the room to his bedside, making as much noise as she possibly could, she flipped the light back on and glared down at him. If he was awakened by her actions, he certainly did a good job of pretending to be asleep. She stalked to the recliner and managed to get it across the room to a position in front of the chair in which she had been sitting. When she had lined up the chairs, she surveyed her work, looking at Roman obliquely, certain that he must have awakened. But she was disappointed. He looked peaceful, relaxed, and soundly asleep. Angrily she switched off the light. Then, taking off her shoes, she put her feet in one chair and slumped down into the other one. She squirmed and wiggled, incensed as she listened to Roman's even breathing and the comfortable rustling sound he made as he turned in his sleep. Twisting and sighing, she tried her best to get to sleep. She was miserable. She had no cover, and her improvised bed had buttons that poked and jabbed her, seeming to urge her toward the real bed.

She took deep breaths and counted hundreds of sheep, but by midnight she had had it. The cool of night had come in, and she lay in her beige dress shivering. And still Roman slept in that big, cozy queen-size bed, snuggled beneath a blanket and a spread.

Unable to endure her agony any longer, she got up and crept over to the bed with the intention of stealing the velvet bedspread. Roman's arms were under the cover, and if she was very careful, Shannon thought that she could take it without waking him. She tugged at the bottom edge, and it seemed to move a little. Again she tugged gently, and it moved a little more. Leaning over the end of the bed, Shannon worked the cover down inch by tense inch until it passed Roman's waist. Holding her breath, she dragged it still closer to her. Suddenly Roman gave a dissatisfied snort, partially sat up in bed, hugged his arms to his body, and then, with a long arm, he yanked at the spread. Shannon had no choice but to release it. Pulling it back up around his neck, Roman succeeded in one quick movement in securing the spread Shannon had worked so hard to get for herself. Shannon was left with nothing to do but slink back to her uncomfortable improvised bed and lie down.

Another hour passed and she was so tired, but also so cold, that she would doze for a few minutes, then awaken shivering. She battled the chairs as long as she could stand it. Then, angry and resigned, she sneaked back over to the big bed and stared down at Roman. Positive that he was sleeping soundly, she tiptoed around to the other side of the bed and very, very quietly eased her weight down on the edge. She stretched out and let a slight sigh of pure relief escape her lips. With extreme care, she slipped under the covers, fully dressed, and lay very still. At last she was warm. She would set her mental alarm so that she could get out of bed and return to her chairs in a few hours. She was sure that Roman would sleep until daylight. By then she would be out of his bed and he would never know that she had bent to his will after all.

Shannon awakened with a start. She was lying on her side, and Roman was curled up to her back, his arm wrapped securely and comfortingly around her waist. Hardly daring to breathe, petrified that he might awaken, she slanted her eyes to look at him, twisting her neck to peer over her shoulder. His wavy hair was in disarray, his long dark lashes closed. Assured that he was still fast asleep, she attempted to slip out of bed after lifting his arm, only to find that several strands of her hair were caught under his head. She eased his arm back down, and turning as much as she could, tugged her hair free, strand by strand. Greatly relieved, she made a hasty escape back to her own "bed." Smiling at having fooled him so cleverly, she settled down, pretending to rest comfortably under impossible conditions. She placed an arm over her face so that Roman wouldn't see the betraying blink of her eyes, and forced herself to breathe evenly. Her charade went on for the better part of an hour. She became so irritated that she felt like walking over and shaking Roman awake.

Finally, at about seven, he began to stir, stretching and yawning like a sleek animal while she peered out at him from under her arm. To her annoyance, he didn't even acknowledge her poor sleeping arrangement. He reached for his towel, slid out of bed and went directly to the bathroom. While Shannon lay there despising him, he dressed and sauntered out as if nothing in the world were wrong. She pressed her arm more tightly against her eyes and listened to his approaching steps.

"Wake up, Shannon. We have a lot to do today. Let's get going," he demanded, shaking her shoulder roughly.

Incensed that he offered no comment on her "bed," she shrugged his hand away and snapped, "You may feel like getting going, but I don't. I slept in these lousy chairs all night because you wouldn't get another bed!"

His eyes raked over her face, and she watched, enraged, as the rigid features softened into a smile. He made a clucking sound with his tongue. "I did invite you to share the bed," he said at length. "And I think you'll get a bit tired of sleeping in chairs. I'm surprised that you didn't get cold." He patted his stomach. "I'm starving. I'm going down to breakfast. Coming?"

Shannon clenched her teeth on a nasty retort. "I have to get washed," she hissed.

While he watched with his arms crossed and amusement showing on his face, she stood up and tried to smooth the kinks out of herself and her dress.

"You hardly look the part of the bride bathed in a honeymoon glow," he mused as she struggled into her shoes. She slammed into the bathroom, where, to her chagrin, she heard his deep chuckle behind her. He was despicable!

After breakfast, Roman and Shannon returned to Blue Haven only long enough to load their belongings into the car and say good-bye to Shirle and Mrs. Angel.

Although Shannon was still angry with Roman, breakfast had improved her disposition, and she decided to make the best of things. She was tied to him for a year, at least, and she couldn't keep her sanity if she was forced into the position of hating him the entire time. Making a concentrated effort to be civil, she questioned him about his home and tried to learn something about his past while they traveled northward.

Though Shannon had lived all of her life in California, she had never taken the coastal route, and she found it fascinating. It was a glorious time of year for a trip. The spring flowers along the hillsides were brilliantly colored, the lavender bushes a mass of violet, the trees lovely. Her eyes were drawn from the vast expanse of ocean to the rolling hills which stretched for miles.

Roman pointed out the various landmarks and areas of interest. When lunchtime came, he told Shannon they would eat in the quaint little village of Solvang, even though it was off the main road. Seeing the storybook village and its authentically styled buildings with thatched roofs and simulated white storks perched in their nests next to chimneys, she was delighted with his choice. She marveled at the gas streetlights from Copenhagen, the stretches of cobblestone sidewalks, the windmills, the restaurants, and the bakeries offering tempting Danish pastries. They ate in a charming little restaurant, and then sampled the rich Danish delicacies before heading back to the coast to continue their trip.

When they reached the beginning of the Big Sur coastline, Shannon gasped. Never had she envisioned such magnificence. "I've heard about it, but I never expected such beauty," she breathed, looking from the ocean sparkling far below the road to the towering pine trees above.

"It is beautiful," he agreed, "and this is only the beginning. Big Sur stretches for seventy-four miles of winding mountain road with the ocean always in view below. It follows the flanks of the Santa Lucia Mountains, which tower four thousand feet above the surf. It's savagely beautiful, but it can also be deadly for the unwary, especially when it's foggy."

As they wound their way around the mountainsides, Shannon could only sit and stare at the ever-present ocean below. The pine trees stood like sentinels, their scent carried by the ocean breeze. The sun was starting to set and the sky was a background of pinks and oranges streaked as if an artist had gone wild with his brush. Shannon thought she would never see anything to equal it, but she lost her heart when they neared Monterey.

Even in the falling darkness, she could see the beautiful white sandy beaches and the twisted cypress and pine trees that graced the land. "Oh, Roman, your city is gorgeous," she murmured, trying to look everywhere at once.

"Monterey was California's busiest and most important settlement until about the middle of the nineteenth century," he told her. "You still see a lot of evidence of the old Spanish and Mexican village today. Eleven of the old buildings are preserved as historical monuments." He drove through the lighted city, giving her a brief tour, pointing out Fisherman's Wharf with its restaurants, novelty shops, commercial aquarium, art gallery, excursion boats and plaza, and showing her Cannery Row, immortalized in Steinbeck's novel. Then they made their way toward their destination, several miles from the city.

The night sky was lit only by moon and stars as they turned down the road which led to Roman's house. Shannon felt her hands grow moist with anticipation. She wasn't sure what to expect. He had said so little about it, but she was anything but disappointed when the house came into view. A beautiful white adobe building topped by red tiles, it sat on a small hill and was surrounded by beautiful gardens and tall trees accented with colored lights. Roman parked the car before a garage, and they walked up the winding walkway to a massive front door.

"Welcome to Casa de Sueños," Roman murmured, the Spanish words deep and smooth on his tongue.

She was just about to ask what the name meant in English when the door suddenly opened.

An old man greeted them with a shy smile. "Mr. Roman . . . madam, it's good to see you. We weren't expecting you, Mr. Roman." His eyes told them that he certainly hadn't been expecting Shannon either.

"Johnny, this is my bride," Roman said, pushing her forward with a hand at the small of her back.

Johnny stared blankly at Roman for a moment before he grinned and declared, "Now, this *is* a surprise! A bride!"

"Could you get our luggage, Johnny, and have Nora freshen the rooms?"

"Be happy to, sir. Carlota has dinner almost ready. Shall I tell her you'll be dining?"

"Yes, that will be fine." Nodding to the man, Roman directed Shannon through a long brick-floored hall to a carpeted spiral stairway. Looking about her, Shannon found the grandeur of the old Spanish-style house enchanting. When they entered a large suite of rooms at the end of the upstairs hallway, Shannon gasped at the sight of the moon casting a golden glow on the waters of the ocean pounding the shore far below the big bay windows.

As though the house had somehow soothed the wild beast in Roman, he smiled warmly at Shannon and asked in a curiously gentle voice, "Would you like to freshen up before dinner? The bath is to your left."

Her own smile was shy and polite. Never had she imagined that he lived in such luxury, not even when Shirle mentioned that he was a well-known artist or when he spoke of his father's racehorses. The rooms were magnificent. Her eyes moved from the large bed, which was the focal point of the room, to the plush blue chairs and deep white carpet. She nodded, then turned to the left.

The bath, too, was elaborately decorated. As Shannon took a cloth and a towel from an ornate cupboard, she heard Roman speaking with Johnny and the woman who must have been Nora. She could hear a flurry of movement in the other room, and she quickly bathed her face and hands and returned to Roman.

Nora and Johnny were already gone, and Roman was stretched out on the bed, his hands beneath his head, his eyes closed. Shannon noted that his handsome face looked a bit weary before her eyes lowered to the broad expanse of his chest as it rose and fell with his deep breathing. When his eyes opened suddenly, catching her staring at him, she quickly turned away. "All finished?" he asked with a sly smile. "Bathing, I mean."

"I know what you meant," she snapped to cover her embarrassment. "And yes, I am finished."

When he stood up, stretching and grinning at her, she couldn't be angry with him. He was so good-looking. And that smile . . .

"Here are your things. If you want to dress for dinner, you may," he said, gesturing toward her luggage.

She realized that she was expected to dress, and she appreciated his thoughtfulness in letting her know. While he went into the bathroom, she rummaged through her cases. She decided to wear a sleek red dress with a square neck and simple lines. Relatively wrinkle-free and neat, it was an appropriate choice for almost any occasion. She had just slipped into it when Roman reappeared, dressed only in slacks. She made a deliberate effort not to stare at his naked chest as she struggled to zip her dress. She had managed to work the zipper at least a dozen times, but this time it jammed and she yanked at it in frustration.

Stepping up behind her, he murmured, "Let me help you." He freed the zipper, then slipped one arm around her waist as he moved the zipper slowly up her back.

"I guess I'm tired," she said, blushing. "I've never had trouble getting the zipper to work before."

His hand stopped moving, leaving her dress half-zipped. His breath was warm on her neck, and it seemed that his lips almost touched her skin. "Are you sure you want me to zip this?" he murmured. "If you like, there's the bed and—"

In an instant she had turned out of his arms. "I most certainly do not want to get in that bed!" she retorted indignantly. She wouldn't be a stand-in for Elleen no matter how legal the marriage was, or how attractive she found Roman to be. She would *never, never* go to bed with a man she didn't love—or who didn't love her.

A half-smile played on his lips. "Shannon, I didn't mean to imply—"

"I know what you did and didn't mean to imply, Roman Morgan!" she snapped. "You've been trying to get me in your bed since the first night we met.

Well, if you think that it will happen now just because I'm here, you can think again. We have an agreement, and I will see that you abide by it. Now, if you don't mind, I'm hungry."

Shannon stared into his eyes, seeing the anger rise in them. He walked deliberately over to the bed and sat down while she glared at him. A muscle twitched along his jaw. "Are you quite finished?" he asked in a low voice.

"Yes, for now."

"It occurs to me," he said, "that the lady doth protest too much. I had no intention of getting into bed with you. You indicated that you were tired. I had intended to suggest that you could take a nap and we could have dinner later. However, since you seem to have had something else in mind . . ." His voice trailed off suggestively.

Try as hard as she could, Shannon couldn't hold his gaze. She felt the heat rise to her cheeks, and she looked toward the window, pretending to study the dark ocean in the distance. What was there to say? She had made a fool of herself again. Why couldn't she learn to keep quiet?

"Shannon," he murmured.

She forced her eyes back to his, hoping he couldn't detect her misery.

"Would you like to sleep awhile before dinner?"

She shook her head.

Standing up, he walked over to the mirrored closet door, pulled a yellow shirt from a hanger and slipped it on. When he reached for a change of slacks, Shannon averted her eyes, again staring out at the ocean. The view was enthralling; she was sure she would find it stunning in the light of day when she was calm enough to enjoy it.

"Ready?" he asked, stepping over to her. Cheeks still red, she nodded.

He led her downstairs and across the brick-floored hallway. Shannon stepped into a marble-floored dining room and looked at the elegantly set dinner table. Then she almost fainted. Sitting there before her were a man who could only be Roman's father—and Elleen.

Chapter Seven

"What are they doing here?" Shannon hissed as Roman touched her elbow when she stopped abruptly.

"They live here," he murmured coolly.

Shannon felt as if the breath had been knocked out of her. "Live here?" she repeated with a gasp. "With you?"

At her barely muted outburst, the other man stood up. "Roman, son, I didn't expect you to return for a couple of months. Come in. Come in. Dinner has just been served. How are you?" His dark gray eyes slid to Shannon's face, and he was unable to hide his curiosity.

Shannon allowed her eyes to skim briefly over his tall form, and she could easily see how Elleen could have fallen in love with him. The only word to describe him was "polished." His head of full dark hair was tipped by just the right amount of gray to make him dashing as well as distinguished. He was tall, lean and tanned. His attire was designed to accent his best features, and his eyes were warm and bright, though piercing. He exuded charm and confidence, and he had a kind of restless animal energy about him. It was impossible to judge his age, but it was only too obvious that he was related to Roman. As Shannon's eyes moved reluctantly to Elleen, observing the cool blond beauty clothed in a white sarong, she thought that she could almost touch the tension in the air. Elleen didn't take her shocked gaze from Roman's face.

"Rome," Roman said, pushing Shannon toward the man, "I'd like you to meet my wife, Shannon." Shannon was sure that he paused deliberately for effect, and she felt like kicking him, but then, she was only there for display, she reminded herself.

Rome inclined his head toward her, and Shannon marveled at his control. "And a beautiful choice you've made," he commented warmly, his gray eyes carefully devoid of surprise, as though Roman returning home unexpectedly with a bride were the most natural thing in the world.

Stepping toward Shannon, he placed his hands on her shoulders and kissed her soundly on each cheek. Before she could catch her breath, he ushered her forward. "Shannon, let me present my own beautiful wife, Elleen. We've only been married a couple of weeks ourselves."

Elleen looked as if she had been slapped in the face. White, tense, stiff, she stared at Shannon. "How do you do?" she mumbled, giving no indication that they had already met.

With the greatest difficulty, Shannon dragged a smile to her lips. "Very well, thank you," she murmured politely, following the woman's lead and not acknowledging that they knew each other.

Elleen made no other comment and Rome pulled out a chair for Shannon next to his own. Roman was left with no choice but to walk around the table and seat himself beside Elleen, opposite his father and Shannon. Not to have done so would have been both rude and obvious.

Rome began the conversation as if the occasion were the most pleasant one he could imagine. "I'm delighted you've taken the step, my boy," he told Roman. "Are you home for good now? Perhaps this beautiful young lady will help you settle down."

It was very hard to see things as Roman had painted them. His father hardly appeared the type to steal his son's girl, and finding him here in Roman's house, if, indeed, it was Roman's house, didn't seem to confirm the hatred that she surmised existed between them.

When Shannon looked at Roman, she found him watching her study his father. "Yes, I am home for good, Rome." His gaze shifted to his father. "And I'm quite sure my beautiful wife can keep me in one spot. Why would I want to roam with such a treasure as this one, and," he added tauntingly, "such a wonderful little family here at home?"

Although Shannon didn't see how Rome and Elleen could possibly miss the pointed words, Rome laughed deeply and lifted his wineglass. "Well said, my boy! This calls for a toast! To the four of us. May our family be a strong and loving one."

Shannon saw Roman's lips curve in a brief smile. She quickly looked away from him and obediently raised her wineglass, tilting it to her lips. What on earth had Roman been thinking of, bringing her here to live with his ex-fiancée and his father?

Shannon didn't miss the way Elleen purposely left her glass on the table, unwilling to drink to their happiness, but no one else seemed to notice. When Shannon looked at the woman's face, Elleen smiled maliciously and Shannon stared into her cold eyes for just a second.

"How did the painting go down south?" Rome asked, smiling at his son as though he were genuinely interested.

"Fine. I painted Lena Lanet again. You remember her, I'm sure."

Laughing as if he and Roman shared a secret, Rome winked at his wife and commented, "Who could forget Miss Lanet?"

Shannon saw the sour look on Elleen's face. Apparently she knew about Miss Lanet, but then, that wasn't unusual, considering that she had also been Roman's model.

"Have you posed nude for Roman?" Elleen asked suddenly, looking at Shannon through her eyelashes, her voice needling. "Silly me!" she hastened to add. "Need I ask? Of course, that must be how he met you."

Shannon worked to keep her voice tightly controlled. "I haven't posed nude for Roman, actually. He rented an apartment in my house. But, of course, you wouldn't know that. I saw you run out of his room one night, but you didn't see me downstairs on my patio." As soon as she had spoken, she knew she had committed some terrible error. Elleen looked as though she had been struck, and the warm, charming smile was instantly wiped off Rome's lips, making his resemblance to his son even more marked. Only Roman seemed amused by her outburst.

"Were you in Newport Beach at the same time that Roman was, dear?" Rome asked, his eyes daring Elleen to deny it. His anger was barely controlled, and Shannon realized that his outgoing personality was a cover for the same ruthless disposition that Roman possessed.

Shannon watched Elleen struggle painfully for the right words, her light laugh pleading for understanding. "Well, sweetheart, you do remember that I went to Los Angeles to visit with Aunt Mary. You know I couldn't possibly go down south and not dine in our favorite restaurant. You did tell me you wanted me to enjoy myself while you were in

Kentucky. You can imagine my surprise when Roman turned up at the restaurant. Then he invited me to see his apartment, and I couldn't very well refuse, could I? I mean he *is* family. And he finds it so amusing to have such a young stepmother." She laughed lightly again, but the sound caught in her throat. "Shannon must have been hiding. I can't imagine why on earth he didn't introduce me if she owned the house where he was staying."

Now it was Shannon's turn to blush. Elleen had put it so aptly. She had indeed been hiding when the woman pounded on Roman's door and later fled in tears. Unable to think of a suitable reply, Shannon simply stared at the woman.

"I see," Rome murmured dryly, obviously not gullible enough to accept the story. He picked up his fork and began to eat. "Mmm, I must compliment Carlota on this beef brochette. It's superb. Don't let yours get cold, my dear." His anger seemed to disappear as quickly as it had come, but Shannon had a feeling that Elleen hadn't seen the last of it. Rome began to talk about his trip and a racehorse he had purchased. Roman and Elleen immediately joined in the conversation, Elleen's comments just a bit too enthusiastic and bright. Because Shannon didn't know anything about racehorses or Kentucky, she smiled and nodded when appropriate, but said very little.

Shannon was relieved when the main course was finished and they all began to eat the pudding that had been provided for dessert. She wanted nothing more than to escape to her room. She hadn't been prepared for what a year of marriage to a man bent on revenge could entail. And she simply couldn't believe that Elleen and Rome lived with Roman. It was unthinkable! He must be a glutton for punishment to want to see the woman he loved with another man right here in his own home. But then, maybe he wanted her at all costs, or maybe he simply wanted to be able to torment her.

Finally Roman stretched and yawned. "Well, if you two will excuse us, it's been a long journey and we want to get settled in. Shannon?" Standing up, he held out his hand to her. For once she was more than happy to go to him. When she reached his side, he wrapped his arm about her waist and hugged her possessively. "Tired, darling?" he murmured, placing a kiss on her forehead.

She hated the way her heart pounded at his nearness, and she tried to manage a casual nod.

"Good night, Rome, Elleen," Roman said, turning to give them a cursory nod before he left.

"Good night," Shannon echoed. "It was nice to meet you."

"It certainly was a pleasure to meet you," Rome said, giving her his broadest smile. "We're happy to welcome you to our family, aren't we?" he asked, turning to Elleen.

Her smile was forced and frigid. "Of course, delighted." Shannon realized that Elleen viewed her as an enemy and the revelation made her shiver.

Walking arm in arm, she and Roman climbed the winding stairs to the second floor. Roman stopped at the end of the hallway and opened the door for her to enter. When he followed her in, she turned to confront him. "Where are your rooms?"

His eyes cynical, he stated flatly, "These are *our* rooms."

"Oh, no, they're not!" she protested hotly. "I want my own room. Surely that's possible in a house this size. There must be ten bedrooms here."

"Seven separate apartments," he corrected. "But

only this one for us. I told you last night that this is
going to look just like a real marriage, and that
includes us sharing a room *and* a bed."

"I won't!" she insisted. "You can't expect me to
live here for a year under impossible conditions. You
didn't tell me all the particulars, did you, when I
agreed to this marriage? Well, I'll just find some
rooms of my own." Turning away from him, she
marched determinedly to the door.

Gripping her shoulders, Roman spun her around
to face him. "Is it such a hardship?" he murmured
gently, catching her unguarded.

"Yes!" she said, raising her head proudly. He was
the one who said it was only a paper marriage. He
didn't want a real wife, so she saw no need to share
his bed like a real wife. And besides, she admitted to
herself, maybe it didn't bother him to sleep with her,
but she had experienced the strangest sensation
when she had awakened with him beside her that
morning.

"I see," he stated, every trace of gentleness
evaporating. "Well, I gave you the chance to get out
of this marriage when we returned from Mexico, but
you didn't care about the details then. I tried to talk
to you, but Jarod had run off, leaving you high and
dry. That put you in a receptive frame of mind,
didn't it? You agreed to a year with me. Do you
think I'll let you back out now?"

"Don't speak as though you're being charitable,
mister!" she snapped. "You didn't do me a favor by
marrying me. I did you the favor, remember? I
wasn't the only one left high and dry! And for your
information, I didn't consider myself discarded and
eager for the first man available. Jarod wasn't the
only man in the world who found me attractive."

When she saw the amused look in his eyes, it
angered her further. "And you neglected to tell me

that you kept your old love right here in the house, didn't you? You didn't mention that you lived here with her and your father."

"What does it matter? My father and I have lived in this house since I was born."

"Where's your mother?" she asked tartly. "Don't you want her to live here with you, too? That would really make the family complete."

Shannon knew she had made an error when she saw the strange look cross Roman's face. "My mother died when I was seven. And I don't *need* my father living here. I permit him to live here because I feel a certain responsibility for him. My mother left the house to me."

She felt the color rise in her cheeks. "I . . . I'm sorry about your mother. How did she die?"

"Late one night I sneaked off on one of the horses we had, and my mother became frantic. She was afraid of horses, but she joined in the search. She was thrown from the horse and killed. My father blamed me. He and I have carried on a love-hate life-style since. He's been married twice since, and he's chased every pretty girl in skirts. He married Elleen because he thought I wanted her. This is the only permanent home he has, and rather than have him keep moving in and out, I invited him to live here with his newest bride."

"Oh, Roman," she whispered, taking his arm in a gesture of spontaneous concern, "that's so sad. You couldn't have known what would happen to your mother."

"Save your sympathy," he muttered brusquely.

She stroked his arm, wanting to soften his curtness. "Is that your well of bitterness, Roman?" she murmured, her eyes misty green as they met his, her lips trembling with emotion for that small child Roman had been. "You can't have had a very pleasant life, living here in the shadow of your father's hatred."

"My father's hatred is his problem," he replied with a measure of calm. "He's a damn fool. I live my own life in the manner I see fit." Suddenly he dragged her to him, tangling his hands in her hair and forcing her lips to his.

She made no move to thwart him, letting him mold her body to his as the kiss deepened.

When he released her, he was breathing hard. "I'm sorry," he murmured. "I shouldn't have done that, but I couldn't resist." A bitter laugh followed. "See what happens to me when I see your vulnerability? You shouldn't waste your sympathy on such a man."

Shannon's own breathing was ragged, her heart beating savagely as she fought to control her emotions. He was only sorry because she wasn't the woman he loved. The woman he loved was downstairs with another man. So why was it that he had only to place his lips on hers to set her on fire? Why was it that her heart was caught between desiring him and despising him? Why did she feel the urge to press her body to his and let him do with her as he would? She licked her lips, pride demanding that she speak harshly.

"Well," she said with some effort, "I won't waste my sympathy on you again, so see that you don't waste your kisses on me!" She averted her eyes to hide the need in them. "Don't use me as a substitute for the woman you love!" There! She had said what was really on her mind. And, she thought with horror, wasn't that truly her only objection?

Roman's eyes turned a dull gray. "You think you're no more than a substitute?" he asked in a low, vibrating voice.

"I most certainly do. You told me you brought me here to discourage Elleen's pursuit, remember?" She laughed bitterly. "I just had no idea how close to you Elleen was. Physically, I mean. You must be desperate to flaunt some woman in her face because she married your father!"

Roman's eyes raked over her. "Don't worry about what I'm desperate to do. You just do your little bit to act the loving wife," he growled, shoving his hands into his pants pockets. "And I'll leave you alone."

"I certainly hope so!" she cried. And she did, didn't she?

Roman walked over to the suitcases which had been stacked on the floor. "Shall I get someone to help you unpack?"

"No, thank you. I can manage. If I must share the room with you, just show me where I can put my things."

Walking to the large closet doors, he slid one back. "The right half will be yours," he commented dryly. "I'll try to keep my clothes off your side." He strode back to the cases and carried them one by one to the closet door. Silently opening his, he began to hang up his clothes.

At his side, Shannon busied herself with her own clothes. When her elbow accidentally brushed his arm she felt as if it had been touched by fire. She couldn't understand the sudden excitement she felt standing there beside him. Somehow the act seemed so intimate, and she despised herself for the way her imagination ran wild. She sighed. It was going to be a long, trying year.

Tersely Roman told her that she could have the top three drawers of the bureau for her things. Then he embarrassed her by stretching out on the bed to carefully watch her while she unpacked her lingerie. His deliberate scrutiny made her jittery. Trying to shove a handful of colorful panties into a drawer, she blushed as the laciest pair tumbled to the floor.

Roman sat up and stared brazenly as she reached for the panties. "Pretty," he commented with a mocking lift of his brow.

Shannon yanked up the bit of lace and snapped, "Don't you have anything better to do than watch a woman put her underwear away?"

With a taunting grin, he shook his head. "I find this very interesting."

"Oh, I forgot," she muttered derisively. "You don't see many women in clothes, do you?"

"More than I want to," he murmured, his eyes raking slowly over her body.

"You really are insufferable!" she cried, throwing the panties at him before she realized what she was doing. To her mortification, he skillfully caught the underwear in one hand.

Her face flaming, she grabbed up a gown and a robe and stalked to the bathroom. She would be damned if she would put on a show for him, and she would be damned if she would share his bed without a fight, too.

When she had completed her bath, she returned to the bedroom, ready to put up fresh objections to having a bedmate. But to her surprise, he was gone.

Though it was only nine o'clock, she was ready for bed. The day had been long and tiring, and she had hardly slept well the night before. She sat down in a chair, struggling to keep her eyes open while she waited for Roman's return. But the minutes passed and she was still alone. The bed looked so inviting. Perhaps he had decided to sleep elsewhere after all. And she was so sleepy. She went to the bed and started to turn down the covers. Then she had an idea that would work as a compromise if he came back.

Pulling off the bedspread, she slipped out of her robe and wrapped the spread around her, mummy fashion, leaving it loose enough for comfortable sleep. Thinking herself sufficiently shielded from Roman's touch should she need to be, she flopped into bed and pulled a blanket up over her bedspread shroud. In seconds she had drifted to sleep, believing herself secure in her cocoon.

She never even heard Roman's return. The first thing she knew, the blanket was whipped off her. Then Roman grasped the available edges of the bedspread and yanked it fiercely upward. Shannon tumbled out of her cocoon like a barrel rolling downhill. Furious at being awakened so rudely, she charged at Roman with fists flying. Then she saw that he was laughing at her, tossing back his head and laughing with abandon! She drew back an open hand to slap him, but he easily captured it in his.

His laughter stopped, and only the twinkling of amusement in his eyes remained. "I told you that we're going to share this bed, and I meant it. And we're going to sleep like two normal people."

"I *am* normal," she hissed, "but I don't know about you. And I refuse to share this bed with you."

Before she had a chance to protest, he lifted her up into his arms, walked back to the bed and tossed her down. Holding her with one arm, he slipped in beside her, pulling the covers up over both of them. "I want to sleep," he said, securing her struggling body against his. "Now, be still."

Realizing that he had made up his mind that they would sleep together, Shannon felt the fight draining out of her. She was so tired and the bed was so comfortable. Lying by him like a wooden Indian, she fought the treachery of her closing lids as she felt his warm body next to hers. Just as soon as he drifted off to sleep, she would make her escape. He couldn't force her to spend the night with him in his bed!

Daylight was brightening the room when Shannon sleepily opened one eye. Not quite awake, she snuggled down cozily under the covers, burrowing deeper as she felt the delicious toasty warmth next to her. Feeling feathery kisses along the back of her neck, she sighed contentedly. A hand touched her breast, and a thrill ran up and down her body. As the caress intensified, a tingling warmth spread over her like fire, arousing her fully. Turning to the source of her pleasure, her eyes opened wide in shock as she realized that Roman was fitted to the contours of her body, his arm nestled beneath her breasts. She had slept with him after all! She started to utter a cry of protest, but she saw that his lids were tightly closed in sleep. He wasn't even aware of whom he was fondling!

She sighed deeply. She had felt so comfortable there beside him that she didn't want it to end. Nor did she want him to wake up next to her as he was, touching her so intimately, and realize that she was enjoying his company. Easing out of his grasp and placing the errant hand behind her, she moved to the very edge of the bed. It was too early to get up, and anyway, she didn't know the house and she didn't want to wander about. As she lay there trying to shut out her confusing thoughts, she slipped back into a sound sleep.

When she awakened again, Roman wasn't beside her. Raising up on her elbows, she looked around, but he was gone. The clock by the bed showed that it was eight o'clock. She might as well face the day; she couldn't sleep forever. Making her way wearily to the bath, she showered. Afterward she pulled on a pair of jeans and a red form-fitting top, choosing not to wear a bra with it. Giving her hair its customary brisk morning brushing, she fluffed it with her hands and shaped it about her face. Then she stood back and stared critically at her image.

She certainly wasn't ready to face Elleen Morgan this morning. The events of the last days had taken their toll on her, and she had already been drained from the strain of Jarod's disappearance. Disappearance indeed! she thought bitterly. While she had been praying for his safe return for twelve tortured months, he had been in the arms of a dark señorita. She turned away from the mirror. She never wanted to think about Jarod again. But he was the reason she was here, and she couldn't forget that. The only time he seemed to be blotted out of her mind completely was when she was in Roman's demanding arms. Then nothing else mattered. Shaking her head, she sighed. That was a situation to be avoided at all costs. She had too much pride to give herself to a man who loved another woman.

Slipping her feet into a pair of soft leather moccasins, she left the room, feeling uneasy in the unfamiliar house. There were no signs of life as she moved down the stairs and across the hall. Wondering where everyone was, she made her way to the dining room. When she reached the doors, she heard voices. She tugged a door open and announced cheerily, "Good morning."

Stepping back in surprise, she hung on to the door. Elleen and Roman stood by the dining-room table, Elleen's arms wrapped about his waist, her head resting on his chest as she murmured something to him. Seeing Shannon, Roman pulled free of Elleen's embrace and stepped away from her, but he needn't have bothered. Shannon had seen more than enough. So he had brought her here to discourage

Elleen's attentions, had he? It was only too obvious that he really had other plans entirely. All at once she was painfully aware of why he wanted her here, and it wasn't to discourage anything. He had brought her to torment Elleen, to make the cool blonde jealous. He wanted his revenge, all right— *and* he wanted Elleen.

"You're up early," he commented smoothly, showing no shame at being caught with the other woman.

"Too early," she retorted. "Or is it not early enough? You seem to have started without me."

Elleen's full red lips twisted into a smug smile and her blue eyes glowed with satisfaction.

"I'll have Carlota prepare your breakfast," Roman said, ignoring her gibe. "Come with me. I'll introduce you."

"Don't bother. I'm sure you're much too busy to worry about a wife." Shannon was trying desperately to control the despair in her voice, but some of it seeped out. This made twice in one week that she saw a man who was supposed to be hers in the arms of another woman. Of course she had known that Elleen was the one Roman loved, but somehow she had believed that he wanted to be rid of the woman as he had said. It was a stupid thing to believe, of course, and she had believed it only because she had wanted to. Why should it matter to her anyway? She knew that Roman hadn't married her for love, and she didn't even like him. It made no difference to her whom Roman loved, did it? Their marriage was only one of pretense, and she knew that he had intended to use her as a weapon of revenge. She knew it, but at this moment, knowing it didn't help. She felt a frustrated anger rise up in her.

Seeing Roman's features harden, she remembered that he had insisted she play the part of the happy

bride. What right did she have to behave so sullenly
with him now? But then, what happy bride would be
pleased to see her groom in the arms of another
woman? And he had said he wanted all the pretenses
of a normal marriage.

Walking to her, Roman linked arms with her and
gave her a brilliant smile. "I said I'll introduce you to
Carlota, darling. It seems that awakening and finding me missing has upset you. Such possessiveness.
Where's that smile of yours?" he taunted with no
warmth in his voice.

Shannon pursed her lips and looked around
thoughtfully. "Well, now, let's see," she retorted
derisively, "I'm sure I saw it somewhere just a
moment ago. Oh, yes. On Elleen's lips, wasn't it?"

Roman's face registered surprise for the briefest
of seconds before he quickly replied, "Come, now,
darling. You aren't jealous, are you?" His lips
parted in an amused smile.

Elleen's smile broadened as she watched Shannon.

Shannon forced her own lips into a smile. "Someone is flattering someone," she replied with sugared
venom in her tone. Turning on her heel, she
marched away, but Roman grabbed her before she
could go far.

"Don't be difficult, my love," he said with false
gaiety, his grip tightening on her arm as he maneu-
vered her back into the dining room and passed
Elleen on the way to the kitchen. Reluctantly Shannon let him lead her into the large, open room. A
pleasant-faced plump woman of Mexican descent
was bustling about the area.

"*Buenos días,*" she said cheerfully. "It is a good
day, no?"

Shannon forced a smile to her lips. "Yes, it is a
good day."

"Carlota, this is my wife, Shannon," Roman explained. "She'd like some of your excellent cooking."

"*Muy bien, señora.*" The dark woman made a bouncing little curtsy. "Let me see. What do you care for? Or I give you a surprise, *sí?*"

"Yes, give me the surprise," Shannon agreed, thinking that one more surprise wouldn't matter.

Carlota patted Shannon's shoulder with a chubby hand. "You go wait at the table." She made a circle with her finger and thumb and winked. "I make your surprise *pronto.*"

Shannon walked with Roman back to the dining-room table and sat down. She was happy to see that Elleen was gone. She couldn't face any more of the blonde's smug looks. Both of them knew that Roman was still in love with her. And the knowledge was inexplicably painful.

Roman took a sip of black coffee, then turned his gray eyes on Shannon. "You didn't give me a chance to explain about Elleen."

"What's to explain?" she interrupted. "Why should you explain being in the arms of the woman you love?"

"Shannon—"

"Just forget it, will you, Roman? If you don't mind, I don't want to hear it. I've had enough surprises for the day. Just do me a favor—when you feel like holding a woman in your bed, get Elleen."

Just then Carlota came bustling into the room. "*Café?*" she asked, setting down a steaming cup. "*Con leche?*"

"Yes, thank you," Shannon replied, grateful for the few Spanish words she knew. Carlota smiled sweetly and retreated.

"After breakfast, I'll show you around," Roman offered, causing Shannon to look at him more closely. Suddenly he seemed attentive and caring, as if he were a different man now that he was on his home ground. Maybe, she reasoned, he was just feeling guilty about Elleen, but she doubted that that was the reason. Guilt seemed foreign to the man. It hadn't seemed to bother him at all that she had caught him with Elleen. She only wished it didn't bother her.

"I don't want to put you to any trouble," she commented.

He gave her a teasing smile. "I'll suffer through it."

She was about to make an angry retort, but Carlota entered the room with a plate of food. *"Huevos rancheros,"* she said, setting the plate before Shannon. "Enjoy, please."

"I'm sure I will," Shannon murmured, looking at the appetizing egg dish. Eagerly she took a bite. It was as delicious as it looked, and she turned to compliment the cook. "Very good."

"Bien. Bien." Carlota laughed lightly. "We feed you good—make you look like one of Roman's models, *sí?"* She made a curvy movement with her hands, winked and disappeared into the kitchen.

Shannon's appetite dulled instantly and she dropped her fork to her plate. She just couldn't seem to get away from Roman's women. The very last thing she wanted was to look like one of them. Realizing that Roman's eyes were on her, she picked up her fork and began to eat again.

"Anything wrong?" he drawled, his eyes appraising her.

Blushing because he must have been aware of the jealousy the cook's words had evoked, she murmured, "No. What on earth could be wrong?" then returned to her meal.

After breakfast, Roman showed her around the

house. It was magnificent, and she was thoroughly
enjoying the tour until they reached Rome and
Elleen's rooms. No one was there, but Shannon
couldn't take an interest in the decor, allowing
herself only a brief glance. When they stepped out
on the sun porch, Shannon was shocked to see
Elleen sunning herself, a book in her hand. Though
the room was sheltered and the sun was out, it was
only nine in the morning and still chilly. Oblivious of
the cool air, the beautiful blonde was stretched out
on a chaise longue in what amounted to two strings
with a few crocheted patches barely covering the
vital spots. Turning, she looked smugly at Roman,
but his face betrayed no emotion. Of course, Shannon told herself, he was used to looking at nudes,
including this one. But how could he maintain his
detached expression when this was the woman he
wanted? The two of them were playing a dangerous
game, and Shannon didn't like being in the middle.

"Enjoying the sun?" Roman asked.

Elleen smiled sweetly. "Yes. I always did love
warm things against my skin. When you're through
showing your bride the house, why don't you join
me?" She looked seductively at Roman for a few
seconds before turning to Shannon. "Both of you."

"Sorry," he replied, faint amusement touching his
mouth. "I have work to do." His eyes moved over
Shannon. "And I won't allow my wife to lie around
virtually naked, as you do, to no purpose." Placing
an arm about Shannon's shoulders, he guided her
back through the doorway.

She heard a cry of outrage behind her and a
sudden thud as the book Elleen had been reading
slammed against the side of the house. Too startled
to comment, she let Roman lead her down the stairs
and out into a beautiful garden. Beyond the garden,

Shannon could hear the waves of the ocean hitting the shore.

As they wandered about the grounds, Roman pointed out his studio, a large, modern two-story building, and the stables beyond. "When I've completed my current painting, I'll show you around more extensively," he said. "The ocean is less than a thousand feet from the wall of the patio. One day we'll explore the rocks down below. There are steps leading to a sheltered cove."

"That would be nice," Shannon agreed, surprised by the offer. Perhaps Roman had some romance in his soul after all.

"Now I must take you back to the house. I'm sorry to neglect my new bride, but this painting really can't wait. It has to be perfect in every detail, and I don't want the image to escape me."

Experiencing a momentary twinge of jealousy, Shannon wondered who the girl was and why she was so special. Then she shrugged the feeling off. It didn't matter who she was, did it?

When they returned to the house, Roman introduced her to the housekeeper, Nora, a sturdy gray-haired woman with a pleasant manner. Leaving Shannon to the woman, Roman went back to his studio. He didn't reappear for lunch or dinner, and feeling a little lost, Shannon retired to her room with a book. When Roman hadn't appeared by ten, she bathed and went to bed.

Only the crumpled pillow on his side of the bed showed that he had slept there when Shannon awakened the next morning. He had vanished again, and she wondered irritably about the painting that was keeping him so engrossed. Or was it really a painting? Elleen was missing from the house much of the time, but then, so was Rome. Shannon dressed and wandered down to the dining room. She was displeased to see that only Elleen was at the table, lingering over a cup of coffee.

"Looking for your husband?" the woman purred maliciously. "He doesn't stay in bed with you very long, does he?"

Shannon didn't think Elleen's comment was deserving of a reply.

"Does he sleep with you at all?" Elleen asked, her blue eyes full of fire. Before Shannon could reply, she answered her own question. "Of course he does. He certainly wouldn't turn down a chance for a sexual interlude, even though you and I both know you're not the woman he wants in his bed. Oh, yes," she continued nastily, "I see right through this little ruse. What kind of fool does Roman take me for? I know that he only married you to get even with me."

"That's not true," Shannon denied, her heart suddenly picking up its beat. She almost added that Roman had married her to stop the other woman's embarrassing pursuit of him, but she realized ruefully that they both knew it was a lie. "Roman loves me," she insisted defiantly, wondering where she found the nerve to give voice to such imaginary nonsense.

Elleen snorted in disbelief. "Love? You simpleton! He's using you to make me jealous. How blind can you be?" She studied Shannon's red face. "Or maybe you're not blind at all. Maybe you think you'll get something out of the deal in the long run." Her striking blue eyes narrowed. "Well, I'm warning you, you make more trouble for me as you did at the dinner table your first night here, and you'll find out what trouble really is. You won't get a thing from anyone then. Do I make myself clear?"

She had certainly made herself clear, but Shannon

refused to be intimidated. Furthermore, she bristled at being called a simpleton! "I have as much right in this house as you do—more, since it belongs to *my* husband," she answered with amazing calm. "I might offer you the same advice. You're married to one man and chasing another. Threaten me again and your husband will hear about more than your trip to Roman's rooms. Do *I* make *myself* clear?"

Plainly surprised by the retort, Elleen stood up and lifted her chin stiffly. "Well, you nervy little thing!" she spat. "You're hardly in any position to talk to me like that. We'll just see who calls whose bluff here!" Spinning angrily on her heel, she stormed out of the room.

Placing her trembling fingers to her temples, Shannon took a deep breath. Elleen's unexpected burst of temper had upset her more than she wanted to admit. She didn't know any of these people; she didn't know what they were capable of doing to her. And her position as Roman's wife was anything but comforting in view of the circumstances. She didn't know if she would have the courage to expose Elleen to Rome in a confrontation, but she had the feeling that Elleen was more than capable of seeing her threat through to the end.

Chapter Eight

Shannon heard footsteps, and she was relieved to see that it was Carlota who was approaching the table. *"Buenos días,"* the dark woman exclaimed exuberantly. "Breakfast for you? Another surprise today?"

Shannon laughed openly. She didn't know if she could stand another surprise after Elleen, but she nodded enthusiastically.

"This is fun, no?" Carlota asked, chuckling as she went back toward the kitchen. Turning abruptly, she called out to Shannon, "Oh, yes, Roman says to say to you that he is painting today. But you are to come to the studio if you like. If you don't like, then he see you for lunch here in the dining room. Okay?"

"Yes, thank you, Carlota." Shannon played with her napkin as the woman vanished. Maybe she should go to the studio and see for herself what kept Roman so busy. No, she decided, changing her mind. She didn't want to watch him paint naked girls, but she had no idea how she *would* spend the day. It had all the beginnings of a dreadful one. Suddenly Rome appeared behind her and leaned forward to brush her cheek with his own.

"Good morning, Shannon. You look lovely today. How are you?" Pulling out a chair, he seated himself beside her.

"Oh, good morning, Rome. I'm fine. I'm just about to have breakfast. It's so late that I thought everyone else had eaten. Roman is painting, I understand, and Elleen just left the table." She was careful not to relate the circumstances which had compelled his wife to leave.

"Good," he said, moving nearer to her. "This will give your old father-in-law a chance to talk with you." He smiled wickedly at her and she noticed his dimples for the first time. She was reminded again of his attractive appearance.

Just as he seemed to expect, she contradicted his "old" comment. "Oh, you're anything but old." She smiled at the glow in his eyes; obviously he resented aging, and he was doing a good job of fighting nature.

"Why, thank you, my dear," he murmured in a deep voice, watching her intently. "It's very kind of you to say such a thing. I'm easily twice your age."

"And Elleen's," Shannon added. As soon as she had said the words, she felt like biting her tongue. She hadn't meant them in the way they sounded at all. She just didn't want to seem terribly young to him, and the words had popped out as soon as they came to mind.

"Ah, yes," he said, smiling just a little crookedly. "But my sweet wife knows more about life than you could ever imagine, I'm sure. Though you must be only a couple of years younger than she is, you've got an incredible freshness and vitality about you." Reaching out a hand, he caressed her cheek. Shannon moved her head in surprise. Roman's comment about his father chasing every woman in skirts came to mind, and she wondered what on earth she was doing here in the midst of this odd triangle. What did Roman want of her? Surely she wasn't to be used as a wedge to drive Rome from Elleen so that Roman could claim her freely! She was terrified that the older man would make a pass at her at any moment.

Shannon had actually thought he loved Elleen, but now she was filled with doubts. Shannon frowned, and Rome's hand dropped to his side.

"I'm sorry, dear. I didn't mean to startle you. You're quite a beauty, young lady, and I'm delighted that Roman found you."

She managed to murmur, "I'm glad too. We're very much in love. I never thought I would marry as quickly as I did." Well, the last statement wasn't a lie, she told herself, even though the first one was preposterous. She certainly hadn't expected to marry like this. She was beginning to see that she had gotten herself into an entanglement with which she didn't know how to cope. She didn't even know where she fit into it. She couldn't simply ignore the situation. And it was becoming obvious that she couldn't ignore Rome.

Taking her hand in his, he said, "Since Roman's painting today, let me show you the grounds. You do ride, don't you?"

"Horses?" she asked.

He laughed. "Yes. Horses."

"I think Roman's planning to show me the grounds himself," she said, wanting to discourage him. "We took a short tour yesterday."

He smiled brightly. "He can still show you whatever he likes. I'll just hit on the highlights today. What do you say? Shall we do it? Will eleven o'clock be all right?"

"We?" she asked, struggling with the word. "You and Elleen."

"No, no," he said, shaking his head as if her question amused him. "Elleen wouldn't be caught dead on a horse. I mean you and me."

She sought an excuse while he waited for her to reply. She didn't think it would be a good idea to go with him, especially without mentioning it to

Roman. Surely he wouldn't really make a pass at her? She must be worrying over nothing. Her imagination was getting the better of her again. A few touches of his hand didn't mean her husband's father would make a play for her.

When Rome placed a hand on her shoulder, she had to swallow a gasp.

"Shannon," he said, frowning at her, "you aren't afraid of me, are you?"

She felt like an utter fool. "No, of course not," she exclaimed, giggling nervously. "It's just that I can't ride," she lied, hoping that she hadn't insulted the man and that the lie would get her off the hook.

His booming laughter filled the room. "Oh, is that all? Well, honey, I can teach you to ride in twenty minutes." He stood up. "I'll call for you at eleven."

Shannon lingered over her breakfast as long as she dared, savoring each bite of a delicious omelet and munching on toast. She was anything but eager to ride with Rome, but she saw no way to avoid it. When she finally did leave the table, she returned to her room and stepped into a pair of boots. She realized ruefully that she didn't want to anger Roman by going riding with Rome, but why should she worry? Roman wouldn't even care. And so what if he did? He didn't mean anything to her, and she certainly didn't mean anything to him. If he really wanted her to play the part of a wife, it shouldn't be odd at all for her to want to make friends with her father-in-law.

She sighed wearily as she walked over to the big window and looked out at the ocean. She *did* care what Roman thought. She surprised herself with this admission. How did she really feel about him? He was certainly exciting—she had always been aware of that. And just recently she had become aware that there was a human side to him. She sighed again and shook her head. It didn't matter how she felt about him, did it? She was, in effect, no more than a guest in his house, even though she had his name. Her life was turning out so differently from what she had planned, and she didn't know what turns it would take from here. Her thoughts drifted to Roman's conversation about his childhood and she felt sad when she again imagined him as a lonely, neglected child.

Shannon lost track of time as she stood there watching the waves wash up on the shore. She wondered if she would ever be able to erase Roman from her heart. How could she just vanish when he was through with her and pick up the pieces of her life as if he hadn't become a part of her? It wasn't until she heard someone walking down the hallway that she shrugged off this peculiar feeling of depression that was threatening to consume her. She walked to the door and reached for the doorknob. It was almost eleven, and Rome would be waiting for her. Perhaps the ride would be good for her after all.

When she entered the living room, he was already there. And, to her displeasure, so was Elleen. At first she had hoped that Elleen would ride with them to ward off any advance Rome might be inspired to make, but seeing the bitter beauty sitting there looking so smug and sure of herself, Shannon regretted the thought. She simply could not like the woman, even had she wanted to try. She drew a deep breath. Elleen wanted both of the Morgan men and she had probably developed a sudden interest in riding when Rome mentioned that he was going with Shannon.

"Ready?" he asked, standing up.

Shannon nodded, looking expectantly at Elleen, but the other woman didn't rise. Instead, she looked at Shannon with eyes full of taunting speculation.

Shannon stepped quickly toward the door. Actually relieved to find herself alone with Rome, she led the way outside.

"Well, let's get on with the day." Rome linked his arm through hers. "The stables are just down the path."

Shannon didn't mention that Roman had already told her where the stables were. To her chagrin, they passed right by his studio on the way. "Want to stop and tell that husband of yours what you're up to?" Rome asked.

Shannon couldn't tell if he meant to be kind or if he wanted to annoy Roman. "No," she said, shaking her head. She noticed the strange gleam in his eyes, and lest he mistake her comment for something which it wasn't, she hastened to explain, "I don't want to disturb him."

A big smile creased Rome's face. "Is that all?" he teased, pinching her cheek playfully with his large hand. "Maybe you don't want him to know you're out with a handsome man while he works."

Shannon fought to hide her exasperation. Rome certainly had a high opinion of himself. "Maybe that's it," she agreed resignedly, hurrying on past the studio.

"Then you do find me attractive," the older man persisted.

Shannon inhaled deeply. "My husband is the most attractive man I've ever known," she said, hoping to put Rome in his place. "And since he looks like a younger version of you, of course I find you attractive."

"More attractive than Roman?" he asked seriously, and though his smile remained intact, Shannon saw his gray eyes darken. Her certainly didn't waste any time in seeing how receptive a woman was to his charms, even if she was his son's bride. But then a man who had taken his son's fiancée could hardly be expected to respect his marriage.

Stopping where she stood, Shannon freed her arm from Rome's grasp and looked him squarely in the eyes. "No man is more attractive to me than Roman. He's the only man I've met who appealed to me so much that I wanted to marry him—and only a few days after we met." She softened the severe statement with a small smile, but she intended for Rome to get her message loudly and clearly. It had sounded so truthful that even she was tempted to believe it.

Unexpectedly, the gleam returned to Rome's eyes. "I'd say that's laying your hand out for anyone to see," he commented, linking arms with her again to urge her forward. "It's even plain to an old romantic fool like me, who sees every pretty girl as a song." He laughed heartily at his remark, and Shannon breathed a sigh of relief. She thought she had just overcome what could have turned into an unpleasant situation. She sincerely hoped that she had made her position plain. She didn't want to be put in such a spot again. The next time, she might not escape so easily.

The stables were some distance from the main house, and Shannon was glad when they reached them.

While she waited, Rome selected two horses and saddled them. When he explained the basics of riding, she pretended that she had never ridden, though she had actually been on a horse several times. It wasn't one of her favorite activities, and she kept her comments light and inquisitive, gratefully stepping into Rome's laced fingers so he could help her onto the horse's back. When she was astride, he handed her the reins and patted her leg. She chose to ignore the latter gesture.

The ride revealed more breathtaking scenery. Shannon could well understand Roman's desire to return here to these beautiful isolated grounds. Rome and she skirted some trees and rode to the edge of an awesome cliff where he helped her down from her horse. Then they stood staring out at the violent ocean as it pounded the shore and the rocks below. Presently they remounted and rode along the path that curved around the estate. As they neared an old private cemetery on the grounds, Shannon saw Rome stiffen. His eyes straight ahead, he stopped his horse and jumped down to stride to a neat, small grave marked by a simple cross. Shannon halted her horse beside his and waited, unsure if she should dismount. After a few moments Rome turned to her.

"This is Maria's grave. Roman's mother," he explained, his voice thick. "I ride out here most days when I'm home."

Shannon stared at the man for a few seconds, not knowing what to say. She could understand loyalty to a loved one's memory, but it annoyed her that Rome indulged himself so, especially now that he had a new wife. She could imagine how Elleen must feel having to compete with Maria's ghost. She was surprised at her thoughts. Why should she care how Elleen felt? She certainly shouldn't feel the need to defend the other woman. Still, as she gave Rome a searching look, she blurted, "I wouldn't like that if I were Elleen."

As though he were astonished by her bluntness, Rome's head jerked up. "You've no idea how much I loved my wife," he said swiftly and bitterly. "You don't know the circumstances of her untimely death, and how difficult it has been for me to go on without her."

Shannon's look was compassionate, but she felt

that the man's grief had been active for much too long. It was unhealthy. "I do know the circumstances of your former wife's death," she said quietly. "And I know of the alienation it created between you and Roman."

"And you think I'm wrong?" he asked scornfully.

Shrugging, Shannon replied, "It really isn't for me to say. But I can imagine how the death of his mother and the guilt placed on him by his father could warp a young child, can't you?" She didn't know why she was saying these things. Roman, of all people, didn't need anyone to defend him. What had gotten into her since she came here? It seemed that both her life and her thoughts had been changed by her association with Roman.

"What are you trying to say to me?" Rome demanded, stalking toward her horse, his body stiff with anger. Strangely, she felt no need to mollify him. He was a grown man who behaved as if twenty-five years of grieving were his right. That it had inflicted scars on his son had only served to satisfy his need to make the boy pay for his thoughtless, childish deed. How it had affected his encounters with the women who came after Maria, and even Elleen, Shannon had no idea.

"I'm not trying to say anything, Rome," she answered at last, looking down into his handsome, distorted features. "I don't know what's in your heart, but hatred brings its own bleak penalty." With that, she turned her horse aside and began to ride away.

In minutes, Rome caught up with her, forcing a tight smile to his lips as he came alongside. Trying to make light conversation, even though she sensed his anger, Shannon commented on the beauty of the surroundings. Rome guided her to the site of an old well, now overgrown with masses of colorful flowers. The spot was gorgeous, and they dismounted to stroll through the knee-high wildflowers and grasses.

Rome bent to pick a daisy and stood by Shannon, plucking off the snow-white petals. "No one ever spoke to me like that before," he said, still smiling uncomfortably as he looked at her. "Do you really think I deserve it?"

Knowing that the very last thing she needed at Casa de Sueños was another enemy, Shannon bit back a positive reply. "I can't see how grief justifies your attitude," she murmured. "We're all exposed to death at some time, but life still goes on for the living. I don't see why everyone around you should be punished for a loss you suffered twenty-five years ago."

Rome flung the flower down and mounted his horse. Shannon followed suit, feeling sure that he would return to the stables immediately, but he continued to show her around the estate, even though he limited his conversation to the scenery. It wasn't until much later that Shannon looked at her wristwatch. She was beginning to get hungry. It was after two, and with a jolt she remembered that Carlota had told her that Roman would join her in the main house for lunch. "Oh, no!" she exclaimed. "I was supposed to have lunch with Roman."

Shannon was certain Rome's look was a gloating one. "And you simply forgot?"

The way he asked the question put her on the defensive. "Yes, I simply forgot. I didn't think of it again, once you mentioned going riding." She could have added that it was all his fault. She hadn't wanted to go riding with him, but she hadn't known how to refuse without upsetting him. Well, it didn't make any difference now. Roman had probably waited for her, growing more angry with the passage of time. How on earth would she explain what had happened?

"Don't look so dismayed, my dear," Rome said. "We'll be back at the stables in a few minutes. I'm sure Roman will understand." But the amused expression in his eyes caused Shannon to think that Roman wouldn't understand in the least. It seemed to say that Rome had won round one of the battle with Roman's wife, just as he had won the war with Roman over Elleen. It also seemed to say that it served Shannon right for her comments about his prolonged grief.

Shannon was certain that Rome deliberately maintained a slow pace as they rode toward the stables. She wanted to urge her horse on, but she was unsure of the way back. She was relieved when they finally reached the building. She couldn't imagine why she was so frantic about the lunch. After all, she hadn't even agreed to it, but she intuitively knew there would be the devil to pay because she had missed it to ride with Rome. She was so preoccupied that she didn't even notice how Rome smiled when he reached up to lift her from her horse, his hands much too tight around her waist. All she could think of was Roman's anger.

Rome seemed to take forever unsaddling the horses and returning them to the stables. Shannon thought that he almost gloried in her anxiety as he went slowly about his task. When he had completed the chore, she hurried off down the path ahead of him, paying no heed to his languid gait as she made her way toward the main house. She didn't slow down until he called after her.

"My dear, there's no need for you to rush. Lunch

was over two hours ago. Roman is sure to be back in his studio by now. If you're concerned about your absence at lunch, we'll stop by and tell him what happened."

That made Shannon feel better for just the briefest of moments. But, thinking better of it, she decided she would rather confront Roman alone. "I don't think that's necessary," she said in a strained voice. "What time does he generally finish painting when he spends a whole day in the studio like that?"

Rome laughed heartily. "Who can tell with painters? It depends on his mood, and," he added, just a bit cruelly, "his model."

"Oh," Shannon murmured, looking up into his eyes. She tried to ignore the teasing gleam, but she was certain that he enjoyed her discomfort.

Catching her by the hand, he forced her to walk at his slow pace. "We'll stop at the studio. You'll be unhappy until you see your husband, won't you? Ah," he sighed mockingly, "young brides."

She didn't want to stop, but she permitted Rome to guide her up the steps and into the main room on the first floor. It was attractively done with modern furnishings and warm colors. Roman wasn't there, and Rome, with Shannon in tow, wound his way up the spiral stairs to the huge room above.

"Roman," he called out.

In the silence which followed, Shannon was sure she could hear her heart beating. Roman didn't answer, but he was sitting before the windows that ran the length and breadth of one side of the room. He was staring out at the grounds below, and Shannon saw that the room had a commanding view of much of the estate, including the grounds where she and Rome had been riding.

"Your wife's here," Rome said. "We've been

riding, and it seems that she's just recalled that you two were supposed to meet for lunch."

Shannon turned and glared at her father-in-law. He could at least have let her do her own talking. For just a moment Roman continued to stare out the window, and Shannon felt her stomach tighten with anxiety. She was totally unprepared for the smile on his lips when he turned to face her, and for a few seconds she was deceived by it.

He strode toward her and placed his hands on her shoulders to bestow a kiss on her forehead. "I did miss you," he murmured, and she felt his fingers bite into her flesh. "But I thought perhaps Carlota had forgotten to give you the message." Both of them knew from his icy eyes and sharp tone that he was lying, but Rome didn't seem to notice.

Looking rather disappointed that Shannon hadn't received the brunt of Roman's dissatisfaction, Rome said lightly, "See, my dear, your worrying was in vain. My son hardly noticed your absence."

Roman's face was a cold mask when he turned to his father. "Next time you intend to enjoy my wife for the day, let me know. I had planned to show her the grounds myself. Don't you have enough to do keeping up with your own wife?"

The bleak expression on Rome's face made Shannon pity him. Of course, she told herself, he knew that Elleen was still making a play for Roman, and it must pain him that the woman he had married still preferred his son. She shook her head, trying to escape the complexity of it all and bitterly regretting her marriage to Roman. She had had no idea how involved and difficult life with him would be, and she hated being in the middle of all the hurt and bickering.

"You seem to have finished painting for the day,"

Rome replied tightly. "I'll leave your wife with you and go to mine." Smiling ruefully, he turned to go.

To Shannon's humiliation, Roman snarled, "You brought my wife here. You take her home."

He released his grip on her shoulders and almost pushed her toward his father. Rome had already turned away, so he didn't see the motion. For that Shannon was grateful, and as she faced Roman, she clenched her teeth, speaking tartly. "No one has to take me home. I can find my own way if you don't want me here."

Roman knew the depth of her meaning, and he arched an eyebrow. "I suppose so," he remarked dryly. "I guess I will take you back to the house myself. It seems to be the only way that I can keep you where I want you."

"And where do you want me?" she asked with asperity.

"As I said, I'm leaving," Rome announced. "See you both at home."

Neither Shannon nor Roman responded, and shrugging his shoulders, Rome left them.

"I asked you a question," Shannon snapped at Roman. "Don't think you can push me around every time something doesn't go the way you want it to. I agreed to this marriage without having any way of knowing what a snake's nest I was getting into. I've just been through a trauma of my own. I won't be used anymore as a way for all of you to get at each other. I honestly forgot about the lunch, and that's that."

Grasping her shoulders in a painful grip, Roman pulled her close to him. "You forgot lunch to go riding with Rome. Next time I leave you word to have lunch with me, see that you do it. I had already told you about Rome and his need for young women. Did you think I was talking for my health, or were you just flattered that he found you appealing?"

Shannon pressed her lips into a thin line, refusing to dignify his question with an answer.

"Well?" he growled.

"No to both questions," she spat at him.

His fingers bit more fiercely into her shoulders and she felt like crying out, but she wouldn't let him know that he was hurting her. "Then you wanted to see how far he would go with you. Is that it? Is your ego still so shattered because of Jarod that you need my father's attention?"

Shannon's anger was rising so fast that she couldn't think rationally. In a moment of fury, she snapped at him, "Ours is only a paper marriage after all, Mr. Morgan. You told me that I was at liberty to do as I pleased with any man so long as—how was it you put it? Oh, yes. As long as I was discreet. What could be more discreet than taking a ride about the grounds?"

Roman jerked her even closer to him, and she felt her breath catch in her throat at the wrath that furrowed his brow. "Did he kiss you?" he snarled. "Or do more than that?"

Even though his fury frightened her, Shannon refused to back down. Some perverse satisfaction in his obvious jealousy made her walk where she shouldn't have trod. "Why do you ask? Couldn't you see clearly enough when you spied on us from your window?"

"I asked you," he growled angrily. "And I demand an answer."

"And I demand that you let go of me," she insisted, the increasing pressure of his fingers causing her to wince from pain.

"Give me an answer!" he ordered, his face much

too near to hers. "You'll give me an answer one way or the other! When I said you could see other men, I sure as hell didn't mean my father!"

"He's a man, isn't he?" she hissed, her eyes dancing with flames of anger.

Suddenly he swung her up in his arms and marched across the room to a large beige couch. Flinging her down upon it, he lowered himself on top of her. Before she could escape him, he began to kiss her, punishing her with his savage caresses. Shannon pressed her palms against his chest and tried to push him away, but he held her too tightly. He reached down to her blouse and pulled. She gasped as the material ripped, exposing her high round breasts to his fiery gaze. His hands moved to caress her with an exciting urgency.

"Stop it!" she tried to cry as his lips moved down her throat, spilling thrills of pleasure as they traveled down to her breasts. She felt a wild fire racing inside her, and her heart pounded dangerously. Her protests died somewhere in her mouth before the words had surfaced clearly. His passion caused her to tremble as he gathered her angrily against his hard body, groaning her name in a tortured voice.

"Shannon. Shannon, my love."

His hands moved across her naked back, and in seconds he had slipped the shredded blouse from her shoulders. Her other garments soon followed. She was intensely aware of the whole length of his body, and as his lips sought hers again, she forgot to fight him. She was vaguely aware of him removing his own clothes, and somewhere in the recesses of her mind the reasons why she should turn from him tried to be heard. She was on fire, and all she could do was answer his demanding passion with her own as he gathered her to him. The pressure of his lips on hers increased, and she felt the sensuous searching of his moist tongue as it traced her teeth and explored the tender contours of her mouth. She moaned softly when Roman lifted his lips from hers to nibble along the length of her pulsating throat. His hands caressed the swell of her breasts, then moved down to sweep across the gentle rise of her stomach. She gasped when his lips found the taut peak of her breast and his hands roamed over her hips as he pulled her more closely to him.

She was devastatingly aware of the long, muscled length of his body, pressing hungrily and demandingly against her soft curves. It arched over hers and she knew Roman intended to take her, but her trembling had turned into an explosion of passion. She lost all sense of fear and shame as she yielded to his love, her desire carrying her on an endless tide of ecstasy.

When his passion had subsided, he rolled away from her abruptly and lay on his back on the wide couch, staring at the ceiling. "I'm sorry," he said in a low, hard voice. "I hadn't intended to do that. I broke our agreement. I promise that it won't happen again." More gently he added, "Unless you want it to."

The pain of rejection suddenly chilled Shannon. She had felt so natural there in his arms, his lovemaking taking her to the border of heaven, giving her unimagined fulfillment. It was obvious that he had experienced no such joy. Now that he had claimed her, he didn't want her. She had disappointed him, she thought bitterly. She wasn't Elleen. "You're right," she said in a choked voice. "You had no right to force yourself on me like that."

Sitting up, he ran his hands through his wavy hair. "I said I'm sorry," he growled. "I can't undo the damage, but I won't violate the terms of our deal again." He slid his legs into his slacks and walked to the small closet to pull a woman's shirt off a rack. "Here. The next time I go to the city, I'll replace your blouse. For now you can return to the house in this." He couldn't seem to make his eyes meet hers, and she quickly turned over on her stomach, numb and sick with shame.

He had made love to her, wishing she were another woman, and like a fool, she had thought it meant something to him. He had used her again. Now, to make her shame complete, he gave her another woman's clothes to cover her naked body. He finished dressing quickly and silently. "I'll see you at the house," he murmured.

Then he was gone, leaving her lying on the couch alone. Shannon clutched the multicolored shirt to her face, determined not to yield to tears. Again and again she opened herself up to Roman, allowing him to make a fool of her, and again and again he did so. This time he had made her the biggest fool of all. He had made love to her and she had wanted him to. And this time she realized that she was in love with him, hopelessly and irrevocably.

Now she knew why Jarod had never been able to set her soul on fire as Roman did. She had never loved Jarod any more than he had loved her. They had been a habit with each other, but they hadn't been in love. They had found warmth and pleasure in their relationship and they had dreamed pretty dreams, but there had been nothing beyond that. She hadn't known what love was until she gave herself to Roman.

She lost track of time as she lay there. She didn't know what to do now. She should just go back home. She should never have come here. But it was too late now. If she faced the truth, she would have to admit that she wanted to stay with Roman. It was humiliating, but it was true.

Darkness settled in and Shannon began to get cold, but the settling chill was nothing compared to the numb feeling in her heart. She had been humiliated when Jarod ran away, but that had been nothing compared to the shame she felt now. She didn't see how she could possibly look Roman in the eye again. It was all his fault; if he hadn't been so angry with her, it never would have happened. Slipping her arms into the shirt, she stood up and pulled on her clothes, then walked to the massive windows. What had Roman seen of her and Rome today as he stood here staring out? Had he seen them at all?

When she heard the downstairs door open, she was startled from her reverie.

"Señora Morgan. Señora Morgan. Shannon," a soft-spoken voice called out. "You are here, no?"

Shannon walked over to the stairs and turned on the light. "Yes, Carlota. Up here."

When Carlota looked up the stairs and saw Shannon, her face filled with compassion. Realizing what a fright she must look, Shannon ran her hands down her face and clothes. Carlota murmured something in Spanish, then said in English, "Roman wants you at home for dinner. There are guests, and everybody waits for you. I think you come now, no?"

Guests! Shannon thought despairingly. Not tonight! "All right," she murmured disconsolately. "You go ahead. I'll be there in a few minutes."

Carlota nodded and left without a word. When she had gone, Shannon stood at the top of the stairs fighting back her tears. So, Roman wanted her at the table, but not badly enough to come for her himself. He didn't want to be alone with her again, but guests for dinner demanded her wifely appearance. She was dusty from the ride and disheveled from her lovemaking with Roman; her clothes were a mess, and the blouse wasn't even hers. Sighing, she smoothed down her hair and stumbled down the steps to find her way out of the studio to the path that led to the house.

The saddest part of all, she told herself as she trudged along, was that she not only wanted to put in a wifely appearance, she also wanted to be a real wife to Roman.

Chapter Nine

Feeling awkward and unsuitably dressed, Shannon walked toward the dining-room doors. Inside she could hear the excited hum of bright chatter. Roman rose from his chair and sauntered toward her as soon as she entered.

"There you are, darling," he said. A warm smile hid the darkness of his gray eyes as he took her arm. "I thought you must have fallen asleep and weren't aware of the time. The studio is conducive to sleep, I know. I've slept there many times myself."

She forced a smile to her lips. "Yes. I was napping, and look at me." She gestured nervously to the colorful borrowed shirt and her red jeans. "I'm hardly dressed for dinner. I had no idea we'd have guests."

Shannon was aware that all eyes were upon her. She looked up to see Elleen, dressed in a stunning pink sheath that set off her frosty beauty. Rome was across from her, smiling at his daughter-in-law's discomfort. A heavy woman in a brilliant orange dress was seated to his right, and a small dapper man sat across from her. Elleen sat between the little man and a rugged, good-looking man in his thirties. Elleen spoke, shattering the uneasy silence.

"Oh, I'm afraid I'm responsible for the dinner guests," she purred, looking suitably contrite. "I got so bored roaming about this house today with everyone gone. Rome took Shannon riding," she explained to the others. The tone of her voice hinted that she had been neglected. "You all know that he can't resist a new face. He has to test his appeal on everyone." She laughed charmingly, and the others joined in. "I just had to have some company. Especially when I went to the studio and Roman was so busy with his new portrait."

Her sly smile caused Shannon's stomach to somersault. Perhaps Roman had not really been angry because of her absence at lunch. Maybe Elleen and he had quarreled.

"Oh, it doesn't matter that you aren't dressed for dinner," Roman broke in, obviously to keep Elleen from saying more. "You look beautiful, no matter what." His voice was quiet and soothing, and even if he didn't mean it, Shannon took comfort from his words. He guided her to the table.

"Maureen," he addressed the heavy woman who appeared to be in her forties, "this is my wife, Shannon." He nodded to the men across from her. "Jacob, Maureen's husband, and Ash, their nephew. These are old and dear friends," Roman explained. "No need at all for you to feel uncomfortable about your clothes. They heard you were here, and when they asked to meet you, Elleen encouraged them to join us tonight." Shannon thought his words sounded a bit cool, but she didn't know who was responsible, herself or Elleen.

Maureen and Jacob made suitable replies to the introductions, but Ash merely smiled at her, appraising her thoughtfully, his eyes saying more than words ever could. It was obvious that he found her attractive, and the thought cheered her. Roman seated her beside Ash and then returned to his chair next to Maureen.

Dinner was served and the conversation picked up again, taking on a lively gaiety. Shannon was re-

lieved to be out of the spotlight, and she responded
politely to Ash's questions about how she liked
Monterey. "I think it's beautiful," she told him,
finding his low voice and warm brown eyes reassuring. "Casa de Sueños is gorgeous. Roman and I
made a brief tour of the city, but I'd like to see it at a
leisurely pace."

"Oh, you don't mean to tell me Roman is neglecting a beauty like you for his painting?" Ash asked.

Shannon shrugged, laughing lightly. "I'm afraid
Roman has been very busy. A new model, I guess.
For a new portrait, I mean."

Looking up just then, she saw that Elleen was
leaning toward them and she knew the woman was
listening to their conversation even though she pretended polite interest in something Jacob was saying.

"I don't see how a new model could absorb
Roman's attention when he has you around," Ash
commented, looking at her thoughtfully. "I'm surprised that he isn't painting you. Or has he already?"
The thought clearly interested him.

Shannon was thankful that she could say he
hadn't. "No, but I must confess that he did want to."

She was surprised to see Elleen lean farther
forward. "You don't need to fib, dear," Elleen murmured with deceptive sweetness. "You're among
friends."

For just a moment Shannon was taken aback. So!
she surmised, Roman had told Elleen about the day
she had agreed to pose for him. What a good little
laugh they must have shared over that. With as much
dignity as she could summon, she replied equally
sweetly, "You're so right, Elleen. I've no need to fib.
I haven't posed for Roman."

"No?" Elleen murmured, a glittering challenge in
her eyes. Then she shrugged and looked away,
allowing Shannon to turn her attention back to Ash.

She should have been relieved that the woman had dropped the subject, but she had an odd feeling that she hadn't heard the end of it.

After dessert, they retired to the living room for coffee. Shannon was escorted by Ash, while Maureen clung to Roman's arm. Shannon didn't even remember Elleen disappearing from the little group, but then, she hadn't been looking for the blonde. No one mentioned Elleen's absence, and when she reappeared with a huge covered painting, everyone looked up to see what she was doing.

"Surprise!" she exclaimed loudly, directing Johnny to set up an easel which he was dragging along behind her. He set it up in the middle of the room, and all eyes turned to Elleen as she hoisted the painting onto the stand and uncovered it. "There!" she cried triumphantly. "This is the painting that Shannon didn't pose for and Roman didn't paint!"

Shannon gaped at it in horror. There she lay on the couch that had been in Roman's living room at Blue Haven, a sad, haunting quality to her eyes, the ribbon still in her hair, and without a stitch of covering anywhere. For a moment she couldn't take her eyes from the painting. Roman had captured her so accurately and so exquisitely, she thought fleetingly. She looked much more beautiful than she considered herself to be. From the corner of her eye she saw Roman spring from his chair and charge toward the painting, jerking the cover from Elleen's hand so violently that he almost knocked the woman to the floor. He covered the painting quickly and removed it from the easel.

He muttered something so low and so angry that tears rose to Elleen's eyes and she spun around and ran from the room. Roman chased after her as if he hadn't finished what he had to say. Shannon quickly followed suit, passing them in the hall and noting that Roman had Elleen by the shoulders and was shaking the life out of her. She heard his angry, scathing voice as she passed them on her way upstairs.

When the bedroom door was closed behind her, she threw herself down on the bed and covered her eyes with her hands. How on earth would she ever face any of them again? Roman had painted her after all! How could he have done that, knowing how she felt about it, and without her permission? He had painted her, and he had shown the painting to Elleen, of all people! What had he intended to do with it? She could just see it hanging in some gallery with men ogling her as they came and went. Seeing herself captured on canvas nude made her feel cheap and vulnerable, and . . . and curiously special and beautiful! She could only lie there and shake her head at her husband's sheer arrogance. The day of the wedding, he had told Shirle and Mrs. Angel that he wanted no one to see her undressed but him. What a fool he had made of her again!

Hearing footsteps in the hallway, she jumped up to lock the door. She was sure it was Roman and she didn't want to see him. She wouldn't see him.

"Shannon," she heard him say quietly. "Shannon."

He could say her name all night, but she wasn't going to let him in.

"Shannon," he said with more intensity. When she didn't reply, he rattled the doorknob. "Shannon, open this door!"

"No," she hissed. "Go away."

He shook the knob with such force that she thought he might rip it from the door. "Open this door before I break it down!"

"Break it down," she snapped. "It's your door!"

"You're damn right!" he growled, but of course, she didn't expect him to do it. Suddenly she heard him throw his weight against the door, and she hurried to open it before he really did break it down.

His face was distorted in anger when he faced her. "I'm sorry about the painting. I—"

"Spare me your apologies, Roman," she hissed. "That's the second time you've been sorry today. I don't want to hear it. I won't hear it. You had no right to paint me. There's no excuse for what you do. There never is!"

He stepped toward her, reaching out to her, and she slapped his face.

For a moment he was livid with rage. He gripped her shoulders and shook her roughly. Abruptly he freed her and stood before her, his face haggard, his eyes brooding.

"What do you want now, Roman?" she asked in a small voice, feeling her heartbeat quicken.

His eyes raked over her face, lingering briefly on her lips. "I want to talk to you."

"Why?" she snapped, his very presence bringing out the anger in her. If she couldn't have his love, she wanted to hate him. She certainly had just cause. "You don't care what happens to me. You've gotten all you wanted from me. There's nothing more to be said."

Roman winced as if she had struck him. Approaching her uncertainly, he reached out to cup her chin, then let his hand drop before he touched her. "Shannon, I told you I'm sorry about the painting. I—"

Shannon took several steps backward. "And I told you before that I don't care about your apologies. I don't care!" she hissed. "Do you hear me?"

Roman's jaw muscles tightened and he clenched and unclenched his fists at his sides. "No?" he asked.

"No!"

"I don't believe you. That's not the answer your body gave me when I made love to you."

Shannon whirled away from him, turning her back to him as she clasped her fingers together in front of her. "How *dare* you?" she shrieked. "How dare you mention that as if—"

Before she could finish, he came up behind her, his fingers digging into her shoulders. With one quick movement he turned her to face him and dragged her forward, his lips grinding down savagely on hers.

Attempting to control the rising strength of her response, Shannon struggled against him. Gathering all of her courage, she broke away. She would not betray herself. She wouldn't give him the ultimate triumph of knowing that she loved him. "Are you satisfied now?" she cried. "You seem to think you can do as you will with me. My feelings don't matter to you. If you want to paint me naked for all the world to see, you do it. If you want to break our bargain and make love to me, you do it. But not anymore. I won't let you use me anymore. I won't be hurt by you again."

When he took another step toward her, she shook her head. "Leave me alone!"

"What will you do?" he queried sharply. "Hide here to protect yourself from anything that might hurt you?"

"You seem to have done that quite well. Why shouldn't I?"

"Just what does that mean?" he growled, his eyes gleaming dangerously.

"You hide, don't you? From your guilt over your mother's death. From your love for Elleen. From everything. Only, you carry your protection around with you, don't you? You keep yourself safe by

nourishing your own bitterness." Shannon was horri-
fied at what she was saying. But, she reminded
herself, she would never have spoken so harshly if
Roman hadn't ruined her life the way he had.

For a long moment he stared at her in silence, his
face a frozen mask of hatred. "What do you know
about it?" he snapped finally.

"I know—"

"It doesn't really matter about me, does it?" he
interrupted. His tone was icy and barely controlled.
"It's you who matters. You and your whims. Tell me,
just what do you want from me now?"

"Nothing. I want nothing from you but that you
leave me alone." She turned her back on him for the
second time.

"That's right," he growled. "You want nothing
from me, but there is something you do want—
Jarod."

Shannon turned slowly to gaze at him in shock.
"You think—" she began.

"He's all you've ever wanted, isn't he? Well, then
by all means, you must have him."

"What do you—"

"I have enough money to afford a good lawyer. I'll
send someone down to Mexico to find him and drag
him back to you. I'll track down the good-for-
nothing petty criminal and give him to you!" He
started toward the door.

Shannon stood absolutely still, choking back her
amazement. It was a long moment before she found
her voice, but then she screamed at him, "I don't
want Jarod! I do not want Jarod! Don't do me any
favors!" Tears came to her eyes and she fought
against them. Jarod! How could the man be so
blind? What on earth would she do with Jarod, when
she was in love with Roman Morgan?

His eyes were glittering when he turned back to

her. "Then what do you want? It can't possibly be my father, can it?"

His suggestion enraged her. She was so furious she couldn't think straight. "All I want is for you to get out of my life!" Tears began to slip down her cheeks. "It's been miserable ever since you came into it."

His eyes narrowed dangerously while he stared at her, and she thought he was going to strike her. "Ah, what's the use?" he muttered savagely. Then he turned on his heel and strode out the door, slamming it behind him.

Shannon sat down on the bed and let her hot tears spill down her cheeks. What she had said was true. All she wanted Roman to do was leave her alone. Offering her Jarod, indeed! And to think that he had actually thought she wanted his father! She was appalled that he would even suggest such a thing! He wanted to be rid of her now; it was all too plain. Making love to her had convinced him that Elleen was the only woman for him. She had to leave his house. She couldn't stay here another night.

Hearing a gentle rap, Shannon whirled around, a sob catching in her throat. "Go away!" she cried miserably.

The knock sounded again, followed by her name. "Shannon?"

It was Rome. She certainly didn't want to talk to him either. Had he come to gloat over her humiliation?

"Shannon, I need to talk to you."

She wanted to say no, but something in his tone caused her to open the door. "There's nothing anyone can say," she murmured.

"Please let me in, just for a minute."

Shannon shook her head helplessly, then reluctantly opened the door.

"I want to apologize for myself and for Elleen,"

he said, his eyes pained. "I'm afraid this is my fault. You see, Elleen still loves Roman."

Shannon looked away from him. Did he think she didn't know that?

"You were right about me," he continued in a flat voice, "when you accused me of using my grief to hurt others. You see, I've taken all my hurt and frustration over Maria's death out on Roman. If I had been home the night he rode off on the horse, Maria would never have gone after him. I felt responsible for her death, and I couldn't face that. I laid the guilt on Roman. Even when I married Elleen, I did it because I thought I was depriving Roman of something he wanted. Now the tables have turned and I find that I really care for Elleen myself." He shook his head sadly, and Shannon didn't know what to say. "I just wanted to let you know I'm sorry you've been involved in our dirty little triangle."

"It doesn't matter," she murmured bitterly, opening the door for him to leave. What had been his real intention? Had he meant for her to know that he was as miserable as she was? He could reconcile himself to a loveless marriage if he wanted to, but she wouldn't stay here while Roman and Elleen carried on their torrid little affair. The confrontation over the painting must have brought all of Roman and Elleen's feelings and motives out in the open. When Rome had left the room, Shannon leaned against the door, breathing raggedly.

She had to get away. If she knew where her suitcase was, she would pack some of her clothes, but she didn't know, and she didn't want to alert the whole household by asking for it. Roman knew where she lived; when sufficient time had passed, she would request that he send her belongings to her.

Reaching for the phone with trembling fingers,

she called for a taxi. She would rent a car and go home. When she had given the address and been told how long she would have to wait before the cab's arrival, she hung up and fell down on the bed. Her thoughts were running riot. She had decided to leave Roman, that much was definite. She couldn't bear to have him know that she was in love with him, but her heart ached at the thought of never seeing him again. It was sad how things had worked out. She guessed she had known all along that she was falling in love with him, but with Jarod on her mind and Roman in love with Elleen, she hadn't wanted to face it. In one way Jarod had done her a favor by finding another woman. In another . . . Although she no longer felt angry with him, she couldn't help but blame him for her predicament. She wouldn't have become involved with Roman Morgan if she hadn't needed money so desperately to find out if her fiancé was alive. She sighed despondently. Maybe it was fate. Love didn't need a rhyme or a reason.

Shannon gathered up her purse, a sweater and several small articles of clothing. Then she opened the door and looked up and down the hall. When she saw no one, she hurried downstairs. She was almost to the front door when Carlota came into the living room.

"Señora?" she asked in a puzzled voice. Her gaze rested on the items slung over Shannon's arm and her eyes lit up alarmingly as the situation dawned on her. "You're not going away?" she cried. "Oh, no! You make a mistake. Roman loves you. I know. He will be very unhappy if you go away."

Shannon smiled ruefully at the cook's confession. Carlota always wanted to please, but of course, Shannon didn't believe her.

"I really must go," she said. "Good-bye, Carlota." Opening the door, she rushed outside, praying that her taxi would soon show up. She was in luck. She had started running down the driveway when the headlights flashed on her. She breathed a sigh of relief when she climbed into the vehicle and gave the driver instructions to take her to a car-rental agency. Then she sat back against the seat and laughed mockingly. Why was she in such a panic? Probably no one but Carlota would even notice her absence—or care.

Shannon's thoughts were churning so fast and furiously that she didn't even know if she was taking the right road. It was very dark and she was unfamiliar with the car she had rented, but putting her foot firmly on the gas pedal, she drove rapidly to the coast highway. She kept thinking that Roman must have wanted to be rid of her very badly to offer to send for Jarod. In fact, he must have been desperate. She laughed bitterly. Didn't he know that all he had to do was tell her and she would have gone out of his life as quickly as she had come into it? Perhaps he thought she would demand the money he had offered her along with the marriage. It proved how little he knew her.

Working herself into despair all over again, she drove mile after endless dark mile. She kept reassuring herself that she would be all right when she reached Blue Haven, but she didn't think she would ever be all right again. She had left her heart in Monterey—with Roman.

When she reached the Big Sur country, she slowed down drastically. She remembered Roman telling her how dangerous the road could be, and suddenly she wished she had waited until morning to leave. She slowed down to a crawl, and still her hands trembled as she gripped the wheel. A car swept up behind her with alarming speed, the head-lights startlingly bright in her rearview mirror. For a moment her heart tattooed wildly, and she wondered if the driver could possibly be Roman. She jumped when it honked impatiently, and she realized that the other driver was angry because she was driving so slowly. She looked for a place to pull over, but she didn't see one. She was too scared of running off the edge of the cliff and tumbling to a certain death in the ocean below to drive farther over to the side.

The driver leaned on the horn again and suddenly darted around her. Another car was approaching in the opposite direction, and the three of them barely missed being involved in a dreadful accident. The impatient driver cut Shannon off to get back into her lane. Startled, her hands shaking, she managed to steer clear of the car, but in doing so, she drove dangerously near the edge of the road. She was too paralyzed with fear to even look to the side. She straightened the car again, but she was trembling so badly that she had to stop at the first wide area illuminated by her headlights.

She was shaking uncontrollably when she put the car in Park. Waiting for her heartbeats to return to some semblance of normal, she sat and clutched the steering wheel. She lost track of time as her thoughts darted from Roman to Blue Haven to the terrible convoluted road and her near-accident. She had no idea how long she had been there when she heard a car screech to a halt behind her. Wide-eyed, she turned to see what had happened. Surely she wasn't in someone else's way. She blinked at the bright headlights.

A man stepped out of the vehicle, and Shannon recognized him as Roman when he slammed the door and strode purposefully toward her, his eyes ablaze in the night. He flung her door open and leaned down menacingly. "You crazy little fool!" he lashed out. "What do you think you're doing now?"

She was nearly speechless, she was so startled. "I . . . I . . . what do you care?" she cried defensively, ashamed that she couldn't even leave him without making a fool of herself.

With one violent motion of his hand, he swept her out of the car and crushed her to his hard body. Shannon was shocked to feel him trembling. "What do I care?" he asked in a hoarse voice. "Shannon, I haven't cared about anything else since the night you rescued me from the ocean. I thought I could give you Jarod if that's what it took to make you happy, but when Carlota told me you had gone, I nearly went mad. I know you love another man, but I want you so badly. I love you too much to let you go," he groaned.

Shocked by his confession, she pulled away from him so she could look up into his eyes. She wasn't sure she had heard him right. "Me?" she whispered, dumbfounded. "You want me? You love me?"

"You must know," he said.

"I must know?" she croaked. "How would I know such a thing? You've been so awful to me."

"*I've* been awful to *you?*" he questioned incredulously.

"You have!" she cried. "You know you have! You've mocked me, taunted me, humiliated me, laughed at me, married me to provoke another woman, let me sleep in chairs, painted me without my permission, and . . . and discarded me when you no longer needed me." She gasped, drawing a deep breath so that she could continue. "I don't even know why you followed me. How did you find me?"

"I told you why I followed you," he almost shouted at her. "I love you. Carlota told me you had gone away in a taxi. The driver's company told me he had driven you to a car-rental agency, and I set out after you. Now, you tell me for what reasons I'm no longer supposed to need you."

"The ones you married me for," she snapped. "I served your purpose in getting revenge against Elleen. You don't need the pretense of a wife any longer."

"I never needed the pretense of a wife," he said in a low voice, his eyes searching hers. "I wasn't seeking revenge, and I could have driven Elleen away at any time if I had been cruel enough, but I hoped that she would be good for my father."

"But you're in love with her!" Shannon cried.

"Didn't you hear what I said?" he growled. "I'm in love with *you*. I was never in love with Elleen. She wanted to marry me so badly that she tried to enlist my father's aid. When that backfired, she married him. Since they found some basis strong enough for marriage, I wanted that marriage to have a chance. I got out of the picture by going to Newport Beach. But I married you because I love you. I told you that story about Elleen because it was the only way I could get you to marry me."

"But I saw you and Elleen in each other's arms in the dining room," Shannon cried.

Roman shook his head. "No. You saw her arms around me, and that was just what she intended. She didn't give up right until the end, but it was never Elleen who stood in our way. It was Jarod. You could think of no one but Jarod. When I found out that you were in love with another man and would never be mine, I thought I would have to be content with painting you. It was the only way I could have you forever, but it wasn't enough. I can't get you out of my system."

Shannon gaped at him. "But you never said

. . . you were always so cold and unconcerned. On our wedding night . . ."

"Do you think I wanted you to sleep in those chairs that night? I was awake the entire time, listening to you, hoping that you would come to me. Did you think I would beg you when you rebuffed me at every turn? I was determined to win your love once we got to Monterey. That's why I asked you to agree to a year. But when I saw you with Rome, I was furious. I couldn't bear the thought that you were interested in every man but me. Jarod had been bad enough. Jarod! I wish I'd never heard that name."

"I don't love Jarod," she murmured. "I thought you loved Elleen, and that's the only reason I went on letting you think I loved Jarod. I even let you marry me knowing you loved Elleen, but I couldn't stay in your house after you made love to me, knowing that you loved someone else. And when she uncovered that picture of me, I wished I were dead. How did she know about it if the two of you weren't still secretly seeing each other?"

"She came to the studio while you and Rome were riding, and she saw that I was working on your portrait. When she told me where you and Rome were, I immediately went upstairs and looked out the upper windows. I didn't work on the picture again; I was too angry. Elleen must have taken it back to the house with her when she left. I didn't think about it again, and after I'd forced myself on you, I felt like such a heel for making a fool of myself over a woman who loved another man that I just wanted to get out of the studio."

Shannon put a finger to his lips. "I love you, Roman. I realized how much when you really made me your wife today."

"You love me?" he asked in disbelief. They were

both silent for several moments. The only sound was the crashing of the surf below.

"Very much," she whispered in a husky voice.

"Oh, my darling," he groaned. "We've wasted so much time making each other miserable when we could have been . . ."

"Could have been what?" she asked breathlessly, leaning close and wrapping her arms around his neck.

He smiled down at her. "You tell me."

Without further prompting, Shannon raised her head until her lips met his. This time his kiss was a gentle caress that gradually deepened. His arms locked together behind her back as he held her close to him.

"Let's go home, Shannon," he murmured. "Home to Casa de Sueños. Rome and Elleen are leaving for good. We'll pretend that this is the first night of our marriage."

"The car . . ."

"We'll send someone to pick it up," he said.

His arm tightened around her waist as he led her to his car. "Casa de Sueños," she murmured. "What does it mean, Roman?"

"House of dreams," he replied in a deep voice, hugging her possessively to his hard body.

"House of dreams," she repeated. "What a beautiful name." And for her, she knew that it truly was a house of dreams. With Roman by her side, all of her dreams would come true.

Silhouette Romance

IT'S YOUR OWN SPECIAL TIME

Contemporary romances for today's women.
Each month, six very special love stories will be yours
from SILHOUETTE. Look for them wherever books are sold
or order now from the coupon below.

$1.50 each

___ #61	WHISPER MY NAME Michaels	___ #80	WONDER AND WILD DESIRE Stephens
___ #62	STAND-IN BRIDE Halston	___ #81	IRISH THOROUGHBRED Roberts
___ #63	SNOWFLAKES IN THE SUN Brent	___ #82	THE HOSTAGE BRIDE Dailey
___ #64	SHADOW OF APOLLO Hampson	___ #83	LOVE LEGACY Halston
___ #65	A TOUCH OF MAGIC Hunter	___ #84	VEIL OF GOLD Vitek
___ #66	PROMISES FROM THE PAST Vitek	___ #85	OUTBACK SUMMER John
___ #67	ISLAND CONQUEST Hastings	___ #86	THE MOTH AND THE FLAME Adams
___ #68	THE MARRIAGE BARGAIN Scott	___ #87	BEYOND TOMORROW Michaels
___ #69	WEST OF THE MOON St. George	___ #88	AND THEN CAME DAWN Stanford
___ #70	MADE FOR EACH OTHER Afton Bonds	___ #89	A PASSIONATE BUSINESS James
___ #71	A SECOND CHANCE ON LOVE Ripy	___ #90	WILD LADY Major
___ #72	ANGRY LOVER Beckman	___ #91	WRITTEN IN THE STARS Hunter
___ #73	WREN OF PARADISE Browning	___ #92	DESERT DEVIL McKay
___ #74	WINTER DREAMS Trent	___ #93	EAST OF TODAY Browning
___ #75	DIVIDE THE WIND Carroll	___ #94	ENCHANTMENT Hampson
___ #76	BURNING MEMORIES Hardy	___ #95	FOURTEEN KARAT BEAUTY Wisdom
___ #77	SECRET MARRIAGE Cork	___ #96	LOVE'S TREACHEROUS JOURNEY Beckman
___ #78	DOUBLE OR NOTHING Oliver	___ #97	WANDERER'S DREAM Clay
___ #79	TO START AGAIN Halldorson	___ #98	MIDNIGHT WINE St. George
		___ #99	TO HAVE, TO HOLD Camp

$1.75 each

___ #100	YESTERDAY'S SHADOW Stanford	___ #106	THE LANCASTER MEN Dailey
___ #101	PLAYING WITH FIRE Hardy	___ #107	TEARS OF MORNING Bright
___ #102	WINNER TAKE ALL Hastings	___ #108	FASCINATION Hampson
___ #103	BY HONOUR BOUND Cork	___ #109	FIRE UNDER SNOW Vernon
___ #104	WHERE THE HEART IS Vitek	___ #110	A STRANGER'S WIFE Trent
___ #105	MISTAKEN IDENTITY Eden	___ #111	WAYWARD LOVER South

Silhouette ❤ *Romance*

15-Day Free Trial Offer
6 Silhouette Romances

6 Silhouette Romances, free for 15 days! We'll send you 6 new Silhouette Romances to keep for 15 days, absolutely free! If you decide not to keep them, send them back to us. You pay nothing.

Free Home Delivery. But if you enjoy them as much as we think you will, keep them by paying the invoice enclosed with your free trial shipment. We'll pay all shipping and handling charges. You get the convenience of Home Delivery and we pay the postage and handling charge each month.

Don't miss a copy. The Silhouette Book Club is the way to make sure you'll be able to receive every new romance we publish before they're sold out. There is no minimum number of books to buy and you can cancel at any time.

This offer expires March 31, 1982

Silhouette Book Club, Dept. **SBH** 7B
120 Brighton Road, Clifton, NJ 07012

Please send me 6 Silhouette Romances to keep for 15 days, absolutely free. I understand I am not obligated to join the Silhouette Book Club unless I decide to keep them.

NAME_____

ADDRESS_____

CITY_____ STATE_____ ZIP_____